POWER GAMES

POWER PLAY SERIES BOOK 1

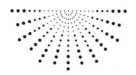

KENNEDY L. MITCHELL

klm

Edited by: Hot Tree Editing

Proofreading: All Encompassing Books

Cover Design: Bookin it Designs

❀ Created with Vellum

To those who strive to be more than who they are today.
You're someone's hero.
Never lose that fight.

ABOUT THE AUTHOR

Kennedy L. Mitchell lives outside Dallas with her husband, son and two very large goldendoodles. She began writing in 2016 after a fight with her husband (You can read the fight almost verbatim in Falling for the Chance) and has no plans of stopping.

She would love to hear from you via any of the platforms below or her website www.kennedylmitchell.com You can also stay up to date on future releases through her newsletter or by joining her Facebook readers group - Kennedy's Book Boyfriend Support Group.

Thank you for reading.

ALSO BY KENNEDY L. MITCHELL

Standalone:

Falling for the Chance

A Covert Affair

Finding Fate

Memories of Us

Protection Series: Interconnected Standalone

Mine to Protect

Mine to Save

Mine to Guard (Coming April 2021)

More Than a Threat Series: A Bodyguard Romantic Suspense

More Than a Threat

More Than a Risk

More Than a Hope (Coming June 2021)

Power Play Series: A Protector Romantic Suspense

Power Games

Power Twist

Power Switch

Power Surge

Power Term

INSPIRATION

"In politics if you want something said, ask a man.
*If you want something done, ask a **woman**."*
- Margaret Thatcher

PROLOGUE

TREY

The big guy is overreacting, if you ask me.

The annoying clicking of keyboards, chattering government employees in the nearby cube farm, and the scent of burnt coffee surround us as we march side by side through the hall toward the director's office. We've been here enough times over the years that the desk jockey's stares don't linger when they glance up from their glowing computer screens. Some of the visits were scheduled, typically follow-ups, while the others weren't so mundane. I have the propensity to find my way into trouble if you ask our director.

My best friend and team lead grunts out another string of curse words under his breath. I can't help the smirk pulling up my lips in response to his pointed annoyance.

I feel great about the stellar life choices I've made up to this point and have nothing to regret. Tank, on the other hand, is on the verge of blowing a gasket if the fiery red tint beneath his dark complexion is any indication. Needless to say, he's still pissed at me, even though I did the right thing. The man can hold a grudge, that's for sure. The incident happened well over twenty-four hours ago, yet he's still pouting.

"If we get fired, I'll murder you with my bare hands, drive your dead-ass body down to Florida, and feed you to the gators. I cannot believe you pulled that fucking stunt."

Yikes, he's cussing. Never a good sign. After this meeting with the director, I should get him something special to make it up to him. I would say a double cheeseburger, but then his wife, Sarah—love her, though I'm scared of her—will ride my ass for feeding him the processed abomination.

I should pick up something for Rachel too. She was fuming yesterday when I told her what happened. No clue why, but damn, she was pissed. *Is* pissed. She wouldn't even talk to me this morning before I left. Whatever it is, we'll either figure it out or I'll apologize and buy her something pretty. That's always worked in the past.

"It'll all be fine like always. Just wait and see, buddy," I mutter under my breath as his thick knuckles pound against the dark wood door separating us from the director's office. "You worry too much."

"Worry?" He turns, facing me full-on. "You tackled the mother-fucking vice president of the United States, you idiot."

I lift both hands, palms out, in surrender. "Listen, I don't mind you plotting my death and telling me about it in detail, but no name-calling. You know it hurts my feelings."

"Of course this is a joke to you. Everything is a damn joke."

On the other side of the door, a muffled female voice yells for us to come in.

Hand on the cool metal knob, I give the flimsy door a push and pause with one foot over the threshold. "If we're going to fight like a married a couple, the least you could do is cook every once in a while, or at least put out," I say over my shoulder with a smirk.

A muttered string of curse words flies at my back as I step deeper into the director's office and pause behind one of the two chairs. Damn, he's fun to rile up. You'd think I would be tired of it after all these years together, but nope, still fun as hell.

Hands tucked in the pockets of my slacks and wearing my signature smirk, I wait for the director to acknowledge our presence. My cocky smirk has gotten me out of more trouble than not, it's worth a shot to see if it can work its magic on her today.

"And what are you smirking about, Mr. Benson?" The director's pinched face peers up from the file flipped open on her desk. The tension in her tired eyes sobers me up a fraction. This could be more of a challenge than I initially expected. Still, not worried, it's me we're talking about here.

"Nothing, ma'am," I respond, still smiling. "You're looking lovely today. Did you do something to your hair?"

"No."

"Something is different. You look ten years—no, make that twenty years younger."

"Cut the shit." She grunts and rocks backward in her high-backed cheap leather chair. An ear-piercing squeak cuts through the otherwise quiet office. She winces as she adjusts, settling further into the leather cushions. "You know why you're here. Let's start with your side of the story, shall we?"

"Short or long version?" I slide my hands out of the silk-lined pockets to grip the mundane office chair's wooden frame in front of me.

"For fuck's sake." Tank stiffens, his back going ramrod straight beside me, shocked at his outburst. Never one to break the rules, that one. It's why we get along so well—I bend the rules to my liking, and he does everything he can to keep me or anyone else from dying. It's fun. "Sorry, ma'am," he apologizes with a slight dip of his head.

The director pulls her thick plastic-framed glasses from her nose and tosses them onto the desk in front of her. "Might as well tell the long version, Mr. Benson. No doubt this will be entertaining."

"Of course." I shift my attention to Tank. "Buddy, you should sit. You don't look so good." It's the truth. His large bald head gleams with beaded sweat, and the buttons of his dress shirt pull taut with each of his deep breaths.

The chair complains under his heavy weight as he sinks onto the stiff cushion. He looks like a cartoon, such a huge guy squished into a tiny chair. Tank's large size came in handy back in the day when he played college football and then went pro after those four years. Nowadays it's the perfect idiot deterrent when we're on the job. Anyone attempting to start shit takes one look at him and bolts in the opposite direction.

"Go on, Mr. Benson. I don't have all day."

"Right, sorry, ma'am." I clear my throat. "Yesterday we arrived at the VP's home, One Observatory Circle, for the start of our shift at eleven hundred hours. Nothing seemed out of place as we made our rounds outside. Inside we met with the beta team in the security office to cover the details of the previous shift: reviewing incident reports, any new threats, checking the VP's schedule for the day, things like that. Inside the security room, movement on one of the screens caught my attention. Zooming in, I recognized the room in question was the library, and inside was Vice President Nick and some woman. They seemed to be talking, but they were a little too close for my liking. Something didn't feel right about the situation, so I left Tank, my team lead, in the security room to see what was going on. When I arrived, I found the door locked, which raised even more suspicion. A loud noise and a muffled shout prompted me to kick the lock and barge in. Once inside the library, I scanned the room, made a quick assessment of the situation, and felt the vice president was in danger, so I handled the situation."

"You tackled a sixty–year–old man," the director says on an exhausted sigh. She seems to do this a lot with me. If she didn't like me so much, she would've canned my ass years ago. Having the Benson family name doesn't hurt either.

"Did Vice President Nick submit a report regarding my actions?" I ask before correcting myself and adding, "Ma'am."

Her pointed annoyed glare says everything I need to know. Of course that limp dick of a bastard didn't write a formal complaint regarding my actions yesterday. I caught him red-handed sexually harassing the woman when I barreled into the library. The director knows all this too. She hates Vice President Nick as much as, if not more than, our team does. Something tells me his hand, along with many other slimeballs' in this city, has found its way to her ass more than once.

Fuck, I cannot wait until the next election. Can't get this asshole out soon enough. Not that the next guy will be any better. At this stage in anyone's political career, they're all the same.

"He didn't, which you know, or you wouldn't be smirking like a kid who robbed a candy shop and got away with it. But dammit, Trey, we can't have our agents tackling dirty politicians any time they feel they're in the right." She lets out an incredulous huff. "There wouldn't be anyone left in DC." A small smile pulls at her lips before she purses them tight. "I've been directed to make an example out of you. Out of the entire team."

Tension tightens my shoulders. The cheap chair frame pops under my white-knuckle grip.

Well, fuck. Did *not* expect this. Accountability? What the hell.

"Gators," Tank grumbles, shooting me a death glare.

"Ma'am, it was my choice. Hell, the guys weren't even around to try and stop me." I jab my middle finger against my breastbone. "Punish me, not them." I may be an idiot at times, but my antics are my own. No way can I live with the team being canned because of my actions.

"You're a team." The chair squeaks again as she leans forward. "You're officially removed as alpha team for Vice President Nick." Her hand juts out, stopping my rebuttal. My lips snap shut, my jaw clenching tight to keep from speaking out of turn. "Beta team will shift into the alpha spot, and Charlie team will replace beta team."

The reality of the situation drops like a lead weight in my gut. I suck in a breath in an attempt to keep a level head. "Ma'am, you know why I did it," I grit out.

Her deep forehead wrinkles smooth a fraction, sympathy seeping into her clear blue eyes. "I do understand, but that doesn't change the impact of your actions. This isn't like your previous antics. You attacked the vice president, and something has to be done."

"Where does that leave my team, ma'am?" Tank asks, voice solemn. Elbows on his knees, hands clasped between them, he drops his head forward.

Double fuck.

"As punishment, your team is now beta team's backup. When the primary elections are finished and the nonincumbent candidates are selected, you will then move back to alpha team for one of the delegates. Dismissed."

The primary election? Nonincumbent delegates?

That's next fall, over a year from now.

I draw in a breath, ready to protest and ask for leniency, but Tank's tight grip on my bicep hauls me toward the door.

"Mr. Benson," the director calls before I'm out the door. Adjusting my suit jacket I turn back toward the office. "The woman, did she press charges?"

Hands fisted, I shove them deep into my pockets. A thick chunk of dark brown hair falls out of place, sliding across my forehead as I shake my head. "No, ma'am, just like the others. Tank tried to talk to her after, but she refused. Said she didn't want to risk her political career over a misunderstanding."

"Misunderstanding. Right." She sighs, her unfocused gaze landing on the wall behind me. "One day I'd love for someone to stand up to these pricks."

The longing in her voice urges me deeper into the office. "Why don't you? You know exactly what goes on behind closed doors." From harassment to bribes and dirty dealings, not to mention all the affairs going on amongst the small political circle, the director knows enough to take down half the men in this city. Then again, those secrets are how she landed this influential role in the first place.

Her perfectly cropped blonde hair swings along her jaw. "No, not me. I'm too deep in this city. I wouldn't survive. Maybe someday someone will come along who doesn't have as much on the table to lose."

Who knows? One day someone could move into this town who still has some morals left and is ready to wreak havoc. But considering I enjoy living, I won't hold my breath for that person to appear any time soon.

CHAPTER ONE

RANDI

APRIL

No. Please no. Not today. I dip my head into the sink and look up into the still-dry spout.

I'm on *Candid Camera*, aren't I?

I glance around the trailer, waiting for someone to pop out and shout, "Gotcha."

Please tell me a friend is pulling a prank. Not that I have friends, but a girl can hope it's all a joke and her water isn't shut off the night before a court appearance. My one paying client needs me at her side tomorrow when the judge gives his final decision on the custody case I've worked on for months. Now I'll look like the low-rent attorney my fees depict me as being.

I twist both the hot and cold knobs, the chipped plastic digging into my palms until neither can turn any farther.

Nothing. Not a single drop.

"No, no, no, no," I groan as quietly as possible to not alert Taeler in the back of the trailer. Can't believe this is happening again. Yes, again. Because this is my reality, and it fucking sucks.

Giving up on the hope that magic water will suddenly pour from the rusted spout, I drop both elbows to the kitchen counter and hold my head between my hands.

Guess the check mix-up scam didn't work with the water company this month. I've pulled it enough times that it's no surprise they caught on to my creative bill paying—or not paying—tactics. I only need three more days. Three days until payday. But of course, some idiot set up a billing system that doesn't coordinate with standard pay cycles. I would file a complaint with the mayor, but said complaint would just end up on my desk.

Yep, the mayor of Boone, Texas, won't have a shower before work tomorrow. Unless I suck up my pride to walk a few trailers down and use Mom's. Chills rake down my spine at the thought. Who knows who her boyfriend is this week, though not a single one is someone I want hanging around while I'm naked, even with a locked door between us. Plus, her place is disgusting, a literal pigsty. As in she has a pig living with her. In the trailer. One of Mom's stupid-ass boyfriends gave her a miniature pig for a gift last year. Turned out it wasn't so miniature but actually a normal size pig, Big Patty, who Mom still refuses to give away.

Taking a small step back, I fall onto the couch. One benefit of a small single-wide is that everything is close. It's not the newest model —okay, it was born before me—but it's mine. Leaks and all.

For now.

Fuck, I don't want to think about that right now. I *can't* think about that right now. If I have to pay the fee to have the water turned back on, plus pay the electric bill on top of Taeler's monthly expenses, there might not be enough to make the full mortgage payment. Again.

My eyes burn with the welling tears. This is my shit show of a life. The life everyone in this small town knew I'd one day grow into. "Once trailer trash, always trailer trash" in most people's minds around here. I'll never amount to anything, and nothing I can do will change that. Well, on that front, yeah, I am proving them right. College and law school, yet I still ended up three trailers down from where I grew up. I like to pretend they aren't smiling behind my back because I'm proving them right each day I sink deeper into debt.

"Mom?"

The skin of my arm peels from my damp lashes as I slide it down. Blinking back the unshed tears, I raise both brows at Taeler.

"Good, you're still up. I wanted a chance to talk to you."

I focus past her shoulder on the dry sink. "Being clean is overrated, right?" I mutter more to myself than to Taeler.

"You are so strange, Mom," Taeler says with a huff, a small smile tugging at the corner of her lips.

"Heads up, the water's off. Something must have happened with a line somewhere. I'm sure we'll be all good tomorrow." Is it considered lying if you're attempting to hide your misfortunes from your kid? I'm going with no.

I groan in utter exhaustion from life and pull myself upright. Puffs of dust and who knows what else float into the air as I pat the other cushion. With all the dramatics of a teen, she flops down beside me. I start to ask what she wanted, but her eyes are glued on the phone in her hand before I can get a word out.

"Did you need something?" I nudge her shoulder with my own, fighting for attention.

Her blue eyes bounce between me and the screen before clicking it off and setting it aside. Once, twice, then a third time she swipes her long blonde hair behind her ear.

Oh no, that's her tell. We both have one. I bite my nails to the quick, and she fidgets nonstop with her hair.

"Mom...."

Shit. This is bad.

"You're pregnant," I blurt before covering my mouth with both hands. My pulse skyrockets with dread.

"What?" She groans. "No! I've told you a thousand times I'm still a virgin, and that's not going to change any time soon. I don't even have a boyfriend."

"Thank fuck," I mutter into my hands. The relief at her denial fades as a new worry seeps into my thoughts. "You're dying."

"Now you're ridiculous."

"What? You're acting more dramatic than usual. It's making me nervous."

"Well, then give me two seconds to explain what's going on."

"You need to speak faster! The suspense is killing me."

"Mom!" she squeaks, smacking a hand over her eyes. "Your first assumptions are pregnancy and death?"

I lift a shoulder in a noncommittal shrug, then circle my hands in the space between us, urging her to tell me what the hell is going on.

"After I graduate next month, I won't... I mean, I'm not—"

I hold up a hand, palm out. "Don't even say it. Not a chance."

"Mom," Taeler pleads, her voice taking on a high-pitched tone. "Just hear me out."

I shake my head and shove off the couch. Her eyes stay glued on me as I pace the narrow hallway. "You're going to school, and that's final."

"I can't afford it. *You* can't afford it."

I flinch, her words a knife to my tender heart.

"It's not your fault," she whispers. Her beautiful blue eyes dance between mine searching, pleading. She stands and grips my shoulders, stopping my pacing. "It is what it is. I'm not upset; I don't feel cheated. You've given me everything you can. I know that. Now, for me, after graduation, it's time to support myself. To be an adult."

"You're not an adult," I grumble. Lifting a hand, I slide my fingers through her blonde hair. We shuffle closer, her forehead finding my shoulder as she releases a long exhale.

"Per the state, yeah, I am. I know you want to change my mind, but you won't." Her words are muffled against my shirt. She's right; I won't change her mind. Taeler is as stubborn as an old mule—a trait she inherited from her father, obviously. "You think I don't pick up on all the stress you're under to pay those crazy student loans each month plus the other zillion bills? I don't want that for me. I'll go full time at the factory after graduation and save up. As I have money, I'll take courses at the junior college."

Lips to her hair, I smile. She's smart, wise even—a trait she received from me, obviously.

"Mom, I know you're behind on a lot of bills, including the trailer payment." Failure settles in my gut like a heavy rock. "I know you're on the verge of losing it, and then what will you do? Live at that crappy office the city lets you use? I'll figure this out on my own, promise. I can't sit back and watch you sink deeper in debt because of me. Please just let me do this, for you."

I tuck my nose into her hair and inhale deeply. "I want you to have so much, so much more than I ever had," I whisper past the knot of unshed tears lodged in my throat. "I'm sorry."

She deserves a better life than this, a mother who can provide more—be more. It's not for lack of trying, that's for fucking sure. I've worked my ass off, yet I'm still here scraping my way through life. I'm utterly exhausted. Nothing I've done is enough to pull me out of the economic status I was born into. I've done what I can for a better life for myself and Taeler, but every time, despite my hard work, I keep failing. Some days I hope for that one chance, one opportunity to prove I'm more than this trailer park, more than an addict's daughter, more than this sleepy town. To ram my success down the throats of everyone who's judged, sneered, and laughed at my hope of breaking the cycle.

I've put in the work, put myself through undergrad and law school, yet the stupid poverty fate gods keep diverting me back to this path lined with bills I can't pay. One would think my résumé, University of Texas at Austin and then on to Harvard Law, would be enough to boost my status, to show everyone in town I'm more than who they judged me to be. But no, that would disrupt the tiny predestined box they want to fit me into.

I press my lips to Taeler's hair, murmuring a quick good-night. My heart sinks as she shuffles down the hall to the single bedroom.

Even with the odds stacked against me, I still have hope. Hope that one day I'll get a chance, that my luck will change for the better. Who knows, maybe the stars will align and I'll get that chance to prove to everyone I'm destined for so much more than this.

And maybe one day I'll have a unicorn as a pet and a genie as a best fucking friend too.

I JAM A RED, indented finger against the On/Off button again and again, each time more aggressively. "Come on, you lazy piece of shit," I curse under my breath. "Work. I'm freezing my tits off here." Still not even a flicker of heat. "I will toss your sorry ass into the closest dumpster if you don't turn on right now," I yell at the ancient space heater.

A click, then the smell of something burning, and finally the rusted metal heating elements flare to life.

Still bent over the contraption, I give it a condescending smirk and a hard pat. "That's what I thought."

"You're talking to the heater again," a female voice croons from the door. "I thought we talked about keeping your crazy under wraps."

Standing tall, I look over my shoulder and stick my tongue out. "Sometimes these things need a reminder of who's the boss around here."

"Right," Jennifer says with a chuckle. "I'm going out for a break. Want to come with?"

Peering through the dirty window of my mayoral office, I catch a tree's green-dotted branches bending in the hostile Texas wind. I walked out this morning without a warm jacket, and it turned out colder than I expected. A Texas April is a fickle time for weather. One day it's beautiful, the hint of spring making you whip out your flops, but then the next, it's bitter-ass cold like today.

"I do, but not outside. Forgot my coat." I glance to the window again and tilt my head toward it with raised brows. "I won't tell if you don't."

A sneaky grin spreads up her cheeks as she nods in agreement. "You're the boss. I can't say no, can I?"

Hands raised, fingers tapping, I let out my best impression of an evil chuckle. "I love all this power."

"Every day you're even stranger." Jennifer gives me a concerned once-over as I shove open the office window. We both visibly shiver as a blast of cold wind swirls into the tiny office. "Are you getting enough sleep? Maybe a lack of vitamin D is making you odd."

"I'm missing D, that's for sure," I say around the cigarette pressed between my front teeth. "I can't remember the last time I had sex."

"What about that guy you met a few months back? Brad... Brian... whatever his name was?"

I roll my eyes and blow a billowing cloud of smoke out the window. "Sorry, I retract the earlier statement from the record. What I meant was I haven't had good sex lately. That guy was a mistake." I shake my head at the memory. "He was super nice and paid for dinner, but he was too...."

"Sensitive?" Jennifer interjects as she leans toward the window, blowing a puff of smoke out into the cold.

"No."

"Hairy?"

"No, he was just—"

"Small in the one area that counts." She gives me a knowing grin. "I'm referring to his penis."

I let out an incredulous laugh. "I gathered that. And no to all that. He was too... handsy."

"Handsy," she deadpans.

"Yeah, too touchy." I shrug as I turn my focus to the glowing ember at the end of the almost-spent cigarette between my fingers.

"Um, Randi, not sure what kind of sex you've had, but I'm pretty sure good sex requires you to be touchy."

Again, my shoulders rise and fall. "He took his time too." My body shakes on a shudder. "Why can't it be good, no-touchy, fast sex? Is that too much to ask?"

"You sound like a guy."

"What? If it takes too long, then my mind wanders, and then I get antsy." I wave my hand dismissively. "So anyway, back to the date. I finished myself off at home that night, then never returned his calls."

"It's a miracle you've ever had an orgasm," she remarks with a snort. Her eyes widen at my one-shoulder shrug. "Randi, please tell me you've had an orgasm from sex."

"Technically?" I glance out the window and flick the now-extinguished cigarette butt into the bucket we keep below for break emergencies like this. "Yeah, I think so, but how do you—"

"Seriously?" a man's voice says, cutting me off. "Typical lazy-ass politician."

I cross both arms across my chest and lean a shoulder against the wall. "Ben." My baby daddy. My first love. My first heartbreak. My first everything. Tall with shaggy blond hair, crystal blue eyes, and solid muscle from working on his parents' farm—how could fifteen-year-old me not fall in love with him? Too bad his aversion to responsibility wasn't as glaring as his good looks.

"Randi," he says with a dip of his chin. "Jennifer. What are you two talking about?"

"Did you know Randi has never—"

Jennifer squeaks into my palm that's quickly suctioned over her mouth.

"Nothing. What are you doing here?" I cringe as a wet tongue laps over my palm. Nose scrunched in disgust, I yank my hand from her lips and wipe my palm down my jeans. Glaring at Jennifer, I shut the window tight. Her unconcerned giggle follows me as I take the two steps back to my chair and fall into it.

"Ah, that." Ben tugs off his ball cap and scratches the crown of his head. "I wanted to stop by, Taeler mentioned she spoke to you last night about her decision on college. Wanted to check in, see how you were doing with her news."

My hands ball into tight fists beneath the solid wood desk. "You knew, and you didn't tell me? How long have you known?"

"She asked me not to," he says, widening his stance and shoving his hands into the back pockets of his jeans.

"Fuck that, Ben," I grit out. Standing, I press both palms on the desk and lean forward. "Co-parenting means we talk about things. We don't keep stuff from each other. I was fucking blindsided. If you would've done the right thing and told me her decision before she talked to me, I would've had a counterargument prepared."

"It's only college, Rand." Ben twists the toe of his worn work boot into the thin carpet. "It's not like going to college did you any good."

True and false.

True, I'm in debt from the various student loans plus the few credit cards I maxed out to cover the daily expenses the loans, grants, and scholarships didn't cover. False that college didn't do me any good. The changes and growth that happen during those years are priceless. It was difficult, and I might have to file for bankruptcy soon, but priceless just the same.

"It's about getting out of here, seeing what the world has to offer outside of this small town." I focus on the peeling ceiling, searching for the right words. "It builds confidence, character—"

"Debt."

"Not everything's about money," I counter with a bit of annoyance in my tone.

"Right." He scoffs. "Look around you, Rand; everything is about money. It's all about who has it and who doesn't. If you haven't looked in the fucking mirror recently, you're in the group who doesn't fucking have it."

"Not yet, anyway."

All three of our heads jerk in the direction of the door, toward the deep, gravelly male voice.

My muscles seize, my lungs forgetting their one job as I lock eyes with the beautiful blue-eyed man. All words and coherent thoughts vanish into thin air. I open my mouth once, twice, but not a single sound makes it out.

Holy shit.

What in the hell is he doing here?

CHAPTER TWO

RANDI

"Miss Sawyer," the coldhearted asswipe, also known as Kyle Birmingham, says. His voice is just as icy and degrading as it was years ago.

My tongue sticks to the roof of my dry mouth. "What... what are you doing here?" I finally manage to squeak out.

Kyle fucking Birmingham.

In my office, of all places.

The last time I saw him, his middle finger was pointed to the sky as he glared at me from across the auditorium after graduation. We hate—nope, that's too soft of a word. We loathe each other. Opposites in every way. We clashed, fought, and debated constantly. This is the very man whose one mission in life those three years was to make my life miserable. There were only a handful of days that I went without breaking down from the constant bullying.

Kyle inspects his suit jacket, brushing off a piece of invisible lint. "I made an appointment."

My gaze darts from him to Jennifer, who's too busy drooling over Mr. Jackass to notice the beseeching look I'm throwing her way.

"Jenn?" I ask. Jenn's been my secretary for the past few years and knows I hate being unprepared, like now.

Her eyes reluctantly swing from him to meet mine, her face morphing into a cringe. "I told you. When you first came in, remember? Someone from his office called this morning demanding I make room on your schedule for someone from their office to meet with you. They never gave a name, just reserved the time slot."

"Oh yeah," I grumble more to myself than Jennifer. Mornings are spent at the small, and failing, family law practice I founded after law school, and afternoons are here acting as mayor for our small town.

"What do you want, Kyle?" Resting back in the rickety chair, I run a hand across my forehead, sealing my eyes shut in an attempt to get my bombarding thoughts together. The asshole is up to something, no doubt about that. If Kyle Birmingham flew from Washington, DC, to our small town, I need to be on high alert.

"You need some coffee or something?" Jennifer asks, her tone dripping in concern.

With a tight, pursed-lip smile, I nod. The silence in the room grows as Jennifer hurries out of the office for the small kitchenette just outside the door, catty-corner to her desk.

"We need to talk," Kyle says, answering my earlier question, cutting his eyes to a tense Ben. "Alone."

"I don't think so," Ben states, nostrils flaring. Have to hand it to Ben; it takes balls not to shrink under Kyle's direct scrutiny. I sure as hell never figured out how to stand up to him.

"It's fine, Ben. Thanks though." I force a fake smile to ease some of the building tension. "I'll hear Mr. Birmingham out, and then he'll be on his way. Right?" My hazel eyes slide back, locking with Kyle's ice-blue ones.

Jaw tight, he inclines his head in acceptance.

Eyes narrowed at the bastard, I blindly take the hot, disposable coffee cup from Jennifer's shaking hand. Still smiling, I motion for her and Ben to give us privacy. One more direct glare from Ben to Kyle, and then the door clicks closed. Kyle takes two steps deeper into the room. His expensive cologne fills the office, burning the inside of my nostrils. He always did put way too much of that shit on.

Lips against the rim of the cup, I take a slow sip of black coffee, peering over the edge to watch him survey the office.

His full upper lip curls. His scowl deepens when his attention falls back to where I sit behind the cluttered desk.

I frown at the minuscule shake of his head.

Not surprising that he finds me and the office lacking. With men like Kyle, nothing is good enough. The Birmingham name is a power-house in Washington, DC. Every member of the family is in some way involved in politics and wealthy beyond anything I can comprehend. He's never had to wonder if he would eat, only when and what. And of course, he's never worked a full day, something daddy dearest ensured by paying for his education plus a generous allowance.

How do I know this?

He constantly boasted of his good fortune, being born into the right family. It added to the various ways he bullied me back in Boston. The day he learned I was Harvard's 'good deed for the century' by allowing someone of my background and financial status to attend the prestigious school, he reminded me and everyone else of the broke scum I was.

His words, not mine.

"Let's get this started, Walmart. I need to get back to the jet before your condemned office falls apart with me in it."

I school my features to hide the blow to my fragile confidence, but the heat still builds beneath my cheeks. I'd almost forgotten the nick-name he graced me with all those years ago. Fucking tool.

"Just get to the point of why you're here so I can tell you to go screw yourself and you can go."

Eyebrow raised, he tsks. The feeble chair wobbles as he settles into the seat. "Nice office."

"Nice face." Well hell. What am I twelve?

"You thought so before."

"I chalk that brief lapse of sound judgment up to a sporadic instance of psychosis. Plus, I thought that before I knew what a gigantic asshole you are."

His cocky smile falters, lips pressing into a hard line. "You and everyone else, it appears," he says with a huff.

"What in the hell are you talking about?"

"We'll get to that in a moment. First, I was surprised when an advisor of mine told me of your status as mayor in this shithole town. I didn't know you were interested in politics."

"Probably because you don't know a thing about me," I hiss, leaning over the desk. "I wanted to make a difference in my hometown." My main drive to come back to Boone was to be close to Taeler after missing so much of her life. A year after I moved home, the local elections came around, and the dumb fuck who'd won the previous cycles, yet done nothing to improve the town, was running uncontested—again. Knowing enough about the ins and outs of being a public servant, I decided to kill two birds with one stone. Be in a position where I could help and be in a position of power to change everyone's view of me.

Only one came to fruition. But hey, at least the few community projects I've spearheaded and after-school programs are successful.

His words finally sink in, smacking me in the face. I hold up a hand. "Why did your advisor even know about me being mayor? Are you keeping tabs on me?" My voice rises with each word.

"I wasn't until a recent development." He leans back in the chair, relaxed hands clasped on his lap. "It was brought to my attention because I need someone like you."

What? I collapse back in the chair, eyes sealing shut. Face to the ceiling, I blow out a tight breath. "I'm imagining all this, aren't I? I've officially sailed from the land of sanity, now floating aimlessly on the sea of lunacy."

"You always were a strange one." I peek one eye open, shooting him an annoyed glare. "It was one reason I hesitated at the mention of you for our plan, but here I am." His eyes flick around the office, disgust written across is perfect features. "You're my only option, or I wouldn't be here, believe me."

"Still not following," I mutter as I rub both thumbs against my temples. There isn't enough Tylenol in the world to hold off the headache this man's presence invokes.

A jostle, then footsteps draw my attention back across the desk. My horny side revels in the way his fit body folds out of the wobbling chair to stand. Long, lean fingers make quick work of his suit jacket's buttons, securing them once again. I chew on a nail as my eyes skim up and down his fancy suit. Damn. He really is beautiful. Silky jet-black hair cut and styled to perfection makes those piercing blue eyes shine, a clean-shaven jaw showing off spotless tan skin, straight nose, and dimpled chin create a Greek god come to life.

No guy should be this pretty. Evolution fucked up with him in so many ways. Why make a man with all that and a greedy black heart?

Yes, his behavior in law school was cruel, but his malicious nature goes deeper than name-calling. He's corrupt greed personified. It's in his arrogant looks, the emotionless aura surrounding him. There's no doubt he would take me out right here in this office if he heard it would benefit him monetarily or advance his career.

But that's a modern politician for you. Kyle Birmingham is one of thousands of corrupt bastards in DC. In that city, it's who can bribe or blackmail to get what you want done for yourself. It has nothing to do with doing right by the American people anymore. Their voice has been forgotten, thrown aside by the politicians assuming their superior mind knows what's best, when they haven't lived a day below the 1 percent—hell, below the upper middle class.

I shake my head to clear the random internal rant. Suspicion and curiosity grow as Kyle paces from one side of the office to the other.

He pauses, turning with his perfectly plucked brows pulled together. "I'm running for president in the next election."

My brows rise and my head tilts. "Congratulations, I guess? If you're here to gain my vote, you won't get it. I'd fill in Betty White as a write-in candidate before I check the box voting you for president of the United States."

"That's why I'm here. The fucking initial surveys say I'm an unfavorable candidate. Can you believe that? *Me*," he shouts. Pacing once again, he runs both hands through his black hair, disrupting the gelled style. "Apparently, the Birmingham name is associated with a dynasty in DC, like we're the damn Kennedys or something. Ignorant voters seem to think it's time for a change."

I raise my hand and nod in agreement. "Not ignorant, aware. I agree it's time for a change in that city."

"Why?" He stops behind the chair, both hands grasping the back as he tilts forward. I hold back from breathing deep as another strong waft of cologne infiltrates my nose.

"Nothing gets done anymore," I say with a held breath. "It's all pomp and circumstance. Nothing is being done to ease the burden on the lower class; instead we're taxed and taxed. All for the sake of more government programs that do shit because the money is mismanaged or whoever's running it doesn't understand the real plight of the American people." Palms down, I push off the desk's worn wooden top to stand. "We need someone who's been here, understands what it's like living below the poverty line and never, ever believing you'll break out of it. Someone who fights for our rights, our freedoms instead of handing them over to some jackass in Washington who thinks he knows better."

My chest heaves, eyes locked with his, tense silence growing with every second he doesn't respond. The wind howling outside the window and the clicking of nails as Jennifer types on the other side of the thin walls the only sounds.

"I one hundred percent disagree with you," he finally says. "But if I want to win the election, I need to embrace these fanatic beliefs. Which—" Kyle clears his throat. "—is why I'm here."

Hell. Either alcohol or nicotine is needed to process this shit and I only have one of those on me.

My legs wobble like a newborn calf as I move from behind the desk to the side window. I snag the pack of cigarettes Jennifer left and pop one between my lips. The window rattles open, a welcomed blast of cold, dry air cooling my heated skin. "You're here to ask me, Walmart, for my help?" Sparks fly from the flint as I flick the lighter twice, lighting the end of my cigarette. "To what, teach you how to have a fucking heart for the American people? To guide you on what it's like to be poor?"

"No." Kyle steps to my side, eyes narrowed at the cigarette. "That's a disgusting habit. And I don't need you to teach me, Walmart. I know who I am, and I know what I want. Adjusting to the voters' perception of me is simply a roadblock, one I already have a plan to overcome. You by my side."

Mid-inhale, I laugh, sending the cloud of smoke barreling down the wrong pipe. Tears well and my stomach tightens at the violent coughing attack it brings on.

"By your side?" I croak, throat raw. I bark a raspy laugh. "You can't be serious."

Right? He's crazier than me.

"I'm offering freedom, Walmart. Don't mock the hand that can save your poor ass."

I grind my teeth, jaw clenched tight.

"Nothing would convince me to help—"

"All your debt paid off, gone." Well, nothing except that. He smirks at my silence, knowing he has my full attention. "I'm talking about changing your life, the life of your kid. Pull your head out of your white trash ass and listen to what I'm willing to offer before saying you'd never partner with me."

As much as I don't want to hear what he has to say, I do. Talk about conflicting emotions. Do I want to stab him with any sharp object within reach, hell yes. Do I also want the chance of a debt-free life for Tae, fuck yeah. I'll give a kidney right here—hell, I'd even cut it out of my own body with a letter opener—to erase all the debt I've accrued over the years. Between student loans, which are currently in arrears, and the few maxed-out credit cards, I'm on the cliff of bankruptcy.

Add in being on the verge of homelessness and recently waterless....

That all sounds great, but at what cost? With men like Kyle Birmingham, everything has a cost. Every word, every move is a power play of some kind in their fucked-up game of life.

"I'm listening." I glare at his bleached-white, straight-toothed, victorious grin. "Begrudgingly, of course."

"Wouldn't expect anything less from you." His features harden as his eyes scroll over me from head to toe. A grimace deepens with each inch his dissecting gaze covers.

I squirm under his scrutiny. Here he is in a thousand-dollar suit—well, that's a wild guess, since I've never seen one before, but with the way said suit hugs his lean frame, there's no doubt it's expensive—and me, well, my dark-wash jeans lost their dark a hundred washes ago. My blazer, a recent Goodwill find, has seen better days, and let's not even get started on my hair. I freaked out at finding a gray hair two weeks ago and hightailed it to the Dollar General for a box of dark brown hair dye.

"What the hell did you do to your hair?"

My mood sours.

"I found a gray hair," I say like it explains everything, but by the look of his furrowed brows, it only explains things to a woman.

"It's the color of day-old dog shit."

"That's oddly specific," I retort, nervously leaning toward the desk as I gather the ugly strands. Grabbing a chewed pencil, I stab the pointy end through the messy bun I constructed and turn back to him.

"A complete makeover will be needed, obviously. Hell, maybe we could find someone to make you somewhat attractive." Those ice-blue eyes narrow as he scans down my frame. I wrap both arms around my waist at the click of his tongue. "Complete wardrobe plus a diet plan and workout regimen. You look like a fucking meth addict." He sighs and rubs the bridge of his nose between two fingers. A clear sheen reflects off his nails. Of course he gets manicures. "Fuck, I can't believe I'm doing this. Grasping at damn straws. Those assholes better be right about all this, or I'll kill them myself."

"You're wasting your breath—"

"All expenses paid by the Birmingham trust. Plus a monthly allowance."

"Allowance," I seethe. "I'll show you where you can shove your allowance, you asshat."

"Ten grand a month."

"Oh, well, uh," I stammer. Shit, that's a lot of money. But again, what's the cost? He's conveniently only covered the perks of the 'help' he needs. "For what, Birmingham? My soul?"

Kyle's chest rumbles, a deep chuckle vibrating through the office. "Basically. All this for your help during the campaign and after."

"After?" I hold a breath. I swear a suspenseful score plays somewhere in the background.

"While I'm president."

I swipe my tongue across my dry lower lip. "And I'm... I'm what? Your advisor on how not to be a conniving, greedy asshole? Not sure there's hope for accomplishing that."

My stomach sinks at the Cheshire grin spreading across his flawless face. Apprehension builds, but no matter what he says, I can't turn down what he's offering. It's a new life. A chance to get Taeler out of this town, to show everyone I can break the cycle.

"No, Walmart. My wife."

Well, except that.

"But I hate you," I respond, each word slow in case he somehow forgot our feud. "And you hate me. Hell, we can't be in the same room without plotting the other's slow death."

Or maybe that's just me. My imagination does tend to lean toward violence.

"Moot point." He shoves both hands into the pockets of his expensive slacks that accentuate his figure. "Most married couples hate each other, but it doesn't matter. I'm talking about you as my pawn, not someone I love." He snorts with one more condescending look up and down. "This offer will change your pathetic excuse for a life. Think about never having to worry about money again, about the opportunities that will be available after the four years. Don't think short term, think about your life, about your daughter's. You want her to grow up piss-ass poor with zero hope of ever rising above the lower middle class, just like her mom, because you're too self-righteous to accept a simple proposal?"

"You asshole," I manage through gritted teeth. Fuck, I hate him. "I know what's on the line. You don't need to remind me of my shitty-ass life." Breaking from his stare, I glance out the window. My chest expands, lungs filling with a deep calming breath to ease the resentment and anger clouding my thoughts.

"Your daughter applied to several colleges and was accepted to a few, yet she hasn't committed to one."

A sharp breath catches in my chest. "How do you know that?"

He waves a perfectly manicured hand in dismissal. "We'll pay for her college too, along with expenses and housing to ensure your... continued cooperation through the campaign and after if—no, *when* I win."

Hell, that's a lot of money in and of itself. Not to mention all the other perks.

"Why?" I blurt. "What can I do as your wife? What does that change for you in the campaign?"

"It eases my image. The people will see I understand their plight, have a voice in my ear from their perspective. With your background, people will eat up the rags-to-riches story you'll tell them. It'll be like saving an injured animal. People will fucking love me."

Oh hell.

He's serious.

But....

The biggest question is, can I do it? Be with him every day, playing pretend wife, all while I hope he dies of a heart attack with no one around to help him? And toss in lying to the American people about Kyle's true self daily, using my shitty history as a talking point in the campaign.

Can I live with being his pawn?

CHAPTER THREE

RANDI

"Jack on the rocks." Exhaustion slurs my words. I slide onto an empty barstool and hold up two fingers to the expecting bartender. "And keep them coming."

This bar is exactly what I need. The other patrons are clustered together in their own booths, leaving the bar entirely empty. It's a local place that used to be busy until the Chili's opened up down the road last year. Now most nights it's like this, a few customers and the lone bartender. It's not updated, but it has stools, booths, and alcohol —all the things a bar needs. Sure, the floors are constantly sticky, the lights are dim, and dust puffs up when you sit on a booth bench, but the happy hour is phenomenal.

I couldn't force myself to go home. Not with Kyle's offer consuming my every thought. I gnash my teeth at the text still on the screen from Taeler. She doesn't want to stay at the trailer tonight—I don't have water after all—deciding to stay with her grandparents instead. They already think I can't take care of my own daughter, and instances like this just prove them right.

Hell, I can barely take care of myself these days.

Maybe everyone is right. I'll never amount to anything. I should just toss in the towel.

I scratch a chewed-up fingernail along my scalp, raking my fingers through my dirty hair. A section of the slick brown strands falls in front of my eyes. I inspect it, holding it up to the light. Damn, Kyle was right. It looks like day-old dog poop. But the box of dye was five dollars, so... it is what it is.

But does it have to be?

I shake my head, swiping the locks behind my ear, and grip the chilled highball glass in front of me. I take a slow sip of the whiskey. The rows of liquor bottles behind the bar blur before me.

Debt free. Plus the monthly ten grand from now until he's out of the White House. All for me. After the 'wife' bomb, he spent the next hour detailing his expectations.

The contract.

I would stand by his side, allow my background to be used as a way to make him seem more human. Pretty much he needs Trailer Park Barbie next to him to show the voters he isn't the aristocratic douche they assume he is at the core. Which he is, so basically I'll lie, which isn't ideal, but no credit card debt and zero student loans to pay back, plus changing Taeler's life, make a convincing argument for hoodwinking the American people.

The last few drops of Jack slither down my throat, leaving a warm burn in their path. The slap of the glass on the smooth wood of the well-used bar signals the bartender for another.

A shadow creeps over, followed by the shuffle of feet to my right. "Celebrating or drowning your sorrows?"

Resting my chin on my shoulder, I flash Ben a tired smile. I should hate him, but I don't. He left me pregnant and scared, let his parents take Tae away from me. A piece of me might love him. Well, maybe not him but the memory of him, of the fun and love we shared before those two pink lines appeared. Maybe when the right man comes along, it'll make me realize my hang-up on Ben is simple infatuation and inability to let go of the past.

The right man. I huff and reach for the fresh glass of whiskey. *Like that will happen.*

In undergrad I was too busy studying and working to date, plus no one wanted to date the single mom. Then during law school, no one would touch me with a ten-foot pole because of the shit Kyle spread around about me. You would think those fancy-schmancy idiots would know poor choices and low economic status doesn't rub off with skin-to-skin contact.

"Both," I say after taking a quick sip as he slides on to the stool to my right.

"Budweiser." The bartender nods before turning to the cooler that holds the longneck bottles. "Do I need to kick that rich pussy's ass?" His smirk grows into a full-on mischievous smile. I love that smirk; it makes me forget to be overwhelmed. "I went to State in wrestling, remember?"

"Yeah, I remember." Mostly because he won't let anyone in a ten-mile radius forget.

"Those were the good old days, am I right?" His Adam's apple bobs with each long pull he takes of the beer.

"Maybe for you," I murmur. "I was pregnant and then had a baby to keep alive and fight to keep."

His shrug has sparks firing in my veins. Idiot. He really didn't get it then and still doesn't. He doesn't remember how difficult it was balancing school and taking care of an infant because he wasn't there. A slice of pain cuts through my heart at the memory of Ben breaking it off after I announced I was pregnant. He loved me but wasn't ready for that kind of *commitment*. Like love isn't.

"I'm sorry for not telling you about Taeler's decision. I really am." His short nails scrape at the bottle's label as he stares at the bar. "But it *is* her decision, and I can't blame her. I know you tried to make something of yourself, but look at you now. Was it worth it?"

All those years separated from Taeler plus the lifetime of debt I accumulated. Was it worth it?

"Yeah it was. Still is." I sigh into the glass at my lips before taking a sip of whiskey. The warmth blooms in my belly, adding to that first glass. For the first time today, I'm not chilled. "At least I know. At least I tried. That means everything. Sure, it's not what I expected, but I'm not giving up, and I feel like that's what she's doing. She's letting a little roadblock stop her from trying. What's the point of living if you don't risk everything for the dream of something better?"

"What did he want, anyway?"

I spin the base of the thin glass on the bar, the remaining slivers of ice swirling together. "A job offer of sorts." A little embellishment never hurt anything. "It could solve all my financial problems, but... I don't know. I hate the guy."

Ben's warm hand wraps around my wrist, stopping the glass. Turning on his stool, he leans forward, putting his face inches from mine. His long blond lashes flutter, drawing attention to his soft baby blue eyes.

"Is he asking you to do something illegal?"

"No." Unless you count lying about his character.

"Did he ask you for favors that involve your pussy?"

I cringe, sliding back on the stool. "So crass."

"Like you have room to talk. Answer me."

"No, he's not looking for sexual favors in return for money, also known as prostitution, which is illegal, which I covered with my 'no' answer to your first question."

"Smartass." The grip on my wrist tightens, sending a shot of excitement straight to my lady parts. What does it mean that a controlling grip gets me hot but a delicate one bores the shit out of me? Hmm, some hands-on research is needed. "I don't see the problem, then," Ben says, turning back to his beer.

My eyes are locked on my wrist, warmth still seeping into my skin from the earlier contact. "Exactly," I muse. "It could be fun research."

"What?" he says, the bottle hovering at his lips.

"What? Oh, sorry, wrong conversation."

"Hope you don't have to pass a psych exam for whatever job he's offering."

Hmm, didn't ask that. Probably should've.

"I'll ask, but this job isn't ideal. I'll lose my voice, my freedom. I'm not sure there's a large enough sum to convince me to give that up. Honestly, I'm not sure I even can."

Ben shakes his head as he angles the empty beer bottle to the bartender.

"I know you can't, baby girl. But I know you tackle anything you set your crazy-ass mind on. If you want more from this job he's offering, then ask for it. Demand it. You've never been shy about demanding what you wanted before. Why now?"

Hmm. Absentmindedly, I chew on a jagged nail. "You speak the truth, wise one."

"Fuck, you're getting weirder as you get older, you know that? You'll end up in a padded room by the time you're forty at this rate."

Five years from now... yeah, he's probably right.

"What's holding me back from telling him what I want?" I ask, more to myself than to Ben. "He told me what he expects and wants out of this deal. Now I need to come up with a counteroffer."

"Surprised you didn't earlier."

Nibbling on my pinky nail, I shake my head. "I was in shock. My nemesis in my office offering to shower me with money and gifts in exchange for my soul was a lot to take in at the time."

"No need to wonder where our daughter gets her dramatics," Ben mutters around the lip of the bottle before tipping it back. "But can I say something?"

I tilt the glass in my hand, indicating for him to continue.

"Why you? I mean, I'm not gay or nothing, but I saw that man, and he's way out of your league."

"Seriously, Ben!"

"What? He's good-lookin' and rich as hell, so what does he want with you? I mean, you're...."

"I'm what, Ben?" I glare into his eyes, wishing mine shot death rays. "You certainly liked the way I looked at one time."

"Yeah, but that was when you were, I don't know, happy? Full of life, maybe. Now you're just haggard."

My jaw drops, my hate-filled glare going with it. "Haggard?"

"Yeah, like life has beaten you down so far that you don't even care to try anymore. Have you looked in the mirror lately?"

I fight a cringe.

"If I were you, I'd have said yes before he had a chance to change his mind."

"I don't want to be someone's pawn."

"Then don't be," Ben huffs, clearly exasperated. "Fuck's sake, woman, isn't that the problem I just solved?"

Gazing into the final sips of whiskey swirling at the bottom of my glass, a poor man's crystal ball, I search for some kind of sign.

"I need to think. Be right back," I mumble over my shoulder as I slide off the wooden barstool. I step through the back exit and immediately wrap both arms around my body. *There goes all that delicious warmth the whiskey provided.* I look to the sky, searching the stars, and snag the pack of cigarettes from my pocket. Movement catches my eye, and I follow Kyle's business card as it flutters in the wind, landing on the gravel a couple steps away.

I snag the small, hard cardstock and flip it over to look at Kyle's handwritten cell number. He instructed me to call, soon, with my answer. But do I even have one?

It's an opportunity to make all my financial worries go away, but at the cost of my pride, my voice, my character. Is there a sum that's worth that?

Ben's right. I need to figure out a way to finagle what I want out of the offer so I'm not the pawn.

Find a way to be the queen in this political chess game *plus* everything he's offering.

But how?

He needs me to make him believable to the voters. What do I want in return? Deep down, it's always been the same—to prove everyone wrong. They think they know me, enjoy the addict's daughter stigma they keep shoving me into. I want to show Ben's parents that I am a good mother, that I can take care of Taeler. It might be a few years later than I wanted, but it still matters to me. Show my teachers, my professors that all the hard work wasn't for not.

A crazy—even for me, which tells you it's batshit—idea forms. One that would give us both what we want. I would come out ahead in my mind, but if it works, he'll be the president of the United States. Not a bad trade-off.

First, am I even qualified?

With a swipe of my thumb across the phone screen I tap the internet icon and type in my search.

Okay here we go.

Natural born U.S. citizen. *Check.*

At least thirty-five years old. *Unfortunately.*

Resident in U.S. for at least fourteen years. *Never even stepped foot in another country, so yeah.*

Nipping the cigarette between my front teeth, I hold out the business card and press the numbers into my phone. Depositing the card back into my pocket, I snag the dangling cigarette and wait for Señor Douchenozzle to pick up. Annoyance rises as it continues to ring. Of course he's not going to answer.

I swipe the screen with as much annoyance as I can channel into my thumb, hanging up on the generic automated voice mail. Just as I'm sliding it back into my pocket, it vibrates with an incoming call. I glance at the screen—Unknown Caller.

Being the one who calls, initiating the contact, is some kind of power play to him, I'm sure. As stupid as it sounds, if this is going to happen, I need to learn the rules of this power game. Fast.

"Walmart." Kyle's deep voice vibrates through the earpiece.

"Tool Bucket," I say on a gritty chuckle. "Get it? You're not just a tool, you're the whole tool bucket." I think I'm hilarious, even if the world doesn't always get my humor.

"Hilarious. What's your decision?"

Right. Decision time.

"Yes, but I want a few revisions to the agreement. I want a voice," I state, pushing as much conviction into my tone as possible. If I don't believe I can do this, there's no way he will either. I have to believe in myself, like I've done my whole life, even with the odds stacked against me.

I can do this. I have to do this. For me, for Taeler, for every person I can help.

"A voice?" Curiosity laces his tone. "Explain."

"I won't accept sitting on the sidelines, allowing you to use me as your poverty puppet to deceive the voters."

An irritated sigh crackles through his side of the line. "I expected nothing less from the only woman who can outdebate me. What does that mean, Walmart? A charity in your name? A fundraiser for the poor? Maybe a building?"

"More," I say, a cloud of smoke billowing out of my puckered lips. I watch it rise into the dark night sky before dissipating with a gust of wind as I wait for his response.

"What, then? What is it that you're asking for?"

Here I go. This is it. My chance to change the tide of... everything. My life and the lives of millions. Just the thought of being able to turn the tables for the working people of this country steels my spine. With my degrees and background, I can be the people's voice in Washington.

"Put me on the ticket. Make me your running mate. The VP." I pause, allowing my words to settle through the phone. "It'll make a bigger impact toward winning the White House. I can do it, I know I can. With me being mayor here plus my law degree, I'll figure it out. I meet the basic qualifications and okay yeah I don't have a lot of experience, but I swear I'll make it work. Hell, even a helmet-wearing monkey is more qualified than the idiot who's in the role currently. Anyone can do a better job than him, and that someone is me."

"You're fucking with me right now."

I shake my head. "No I'm not. I won't be Poverty Barbie who you can flounce around as your good deed. If you want the White House, if you want the most powerful position in the world, then list me as the vice president. I know it's a crazy idea but what do you have to lose? It's either this or nothing for me."

Nothing. His deep breaths huffing across the mouthpiece are the only indication he's still on the line. The silence is a good sign. It means he's considering it, not telling me to fuck off and ending the call. If he's not considering it, then I've fucked over my daughter's future. No pressure.

I rake a couple fingers through my nasty, dirty hair. A minute passes of deafening silence. I bob on the balls of my feet, attempting to get some feeling back in my toes.

"I'm inclined to tell you to fuck off and watch you fail miserably at life, but if I say yes to your proposal, then I'll have a front row seat to your failure here in DC."

"I won't fail." I flick the cigarette butt to the ground and grind it into the gray gravel with the toe of my shoe. No way. Not happening. This is my shot to get ahead, to prove to everyone, prove to myself, that I'm more than what I was born into.

His condescending laugh rattles through the phone, and my upper lip curls in a snarl. "Oh, but you will, Walmart. You think you can play with the most powerful people in the world and win with no experience? I'm questioning your intelligence. They will chew you up before you even start the campaign."

"Aw," I coo, faking surprise. "You do care about me."

"I care about winning. Tell you what. I'll pitch your ludicrous proposal to my advisors and campaign manager. I'll send for you when I know more. Just to make sure I understand this correctly, it's either the vice president position or nothing. Correct?"

"Correct." I swallow hard against the knot building in my throat.

"If I propose this, there's no going back. If we lose, there will be no ongoing funds since you won't be my legal wife. Understand?"

"Yes, yes, I understand everything, Kyle." Shit, didn't think about that side effect. If we do this, it means we have to win.

"Also know that the man who's currently slated as my running mate will not be happy if he's kicked off the ticket. If this does work, know you'll have a target on your back."

That's mysteriously ominous.

I open my mouth to ask what he means but snap it shut at the void on the other end of the phone. Peeling it from my ear, I scan the black screen and let out an incredulous snort. Of course the douche hung up on me.

Tapping the edge of the phone against my thigh, I again stare up into the dark night sky. My pulse races as the reality of the situation sinks deep.

I'm crazier than anyone gives me credit for. Vice president? For fuck's sake.

"Damn idiot," I mutter.

Now I wait and maybe run by Mom's to take a shower.

Hand wrapped around the cold metal handle, I give it a hard tug, swinging the exit door open. Laughter and old country music fill the hall as I make my way back to the bar. With every step, the same two questions repeat over and over in my mind.

What will I do if he says yes?

What will I do if he says no?

CHAPTER FOUR

RANDI

The wheels of my rolling suitcase quietly whirl down the carpeted hall. Fancy chandeliers dot the long hallway's ceiling, making the suite of offices appear like a hotel rather than a place of business. Of course, I am in Washington, DC. Maybe people use this space for business and pleasure; the two go hand in hand in our nation's capital, after all.

Wait. I tilt my nose and inhale deep. *Is that vanilla?*

Midstep I halt, sniffing the air. Surely this building isn't piping a yummy scent into their hallways. I spin, eyes falling to the floral wallpaper. What if the wallpaper is scented and that's what I'm smelling? That would be opulent fancy. I cut my eyes both ways, making sure the coast is clear, and lean toward to the wall. The wallpaper brushes the tip of my nose, but the delectable scent isn't any stronger than when I was a few feet away.

Unless… it could be scratch and sniff—I saw that in a movie once. Forgetting my surroundings, my sole focus on the scent mystery, I scratch a mauve flower with the edge of my serrated nail. Nose pressed firmly to the same spot, I sniff.

"What the hell are you doing?"

Startled, I jolt back, my hand catching the extended handle of my rolling suitcase. It teeters before falling to the floor with an echoing thump.

I shift from one heel to the other, avoiding the man's pointed glare.

"Smelling the wall." I frown at my ragged bag on the pristine carpet. "The scent in the hall... I thought it came from the wallpaper, so I sniffed it. I'm sure it happens all the time." My knees pop as I squat, righting the toppled suitcase.

"I can guarantee you it doesn't. Kyle mentioned you were a strange one." His near-black eyes flick to his watch, a frown forming.

Using the distraction, I take in the rude man. Dirty-blond hair, square jaw with high cheekbones, and a narrow upturned nose. Attractive if it weren't for the dark and foreboding aura pulsing around him. Every internal alarm sounds, the clenching in my gut telling me to get the hell out of here.

His eyes swing back to me, narrowing. "Hurry up. You're late."

I tighten my grip on the suitcase handle, the hard plastic slipping in my sweat-damp palm.

My steps are hesitant, the bag barely rolling behind me. "I'm at a disadvantage. Who are you?"

An unnaturally wide smile curls up his cheeks, and I retreat a step. He appeared dangerous before, but with this Joker-like smile, I'm sufficiently creeped out.

"Come on, Trailer." He shoves off the thick, dark wood door without a glance back, moving into the office suite.

"Asshat," I grumble under my breath. I grip the door's edge before it closes. Shoving it open, I lug the bag through, only for it to close sooner than I expect. Near my limit for the day, I hold back a scream of frustration. Backtracking, I give the heavy door another big shove, freeing my suitcase. Sweat beads beneath my arms and glistens on my forehead. Hopefully I don't look as discombobulated as I feel. The redeye flight out of DFW was rough in its own right. Add in the constant turbulence from there to DC, then the frantic scene at the taxi stand at Reagan and I'm whipped.

"Good to see you finally made it, Walmart." Kyle sneers as I cough at the assault of his overpowering cologne. "Come, we have items to discuss."

I swallow, fighting the panic that wants to seal off my airway as I follow him into the next room. Yesterday, Kyle called, informing me they'd come to a decision on my counteroffer and I was needed in DC as soon as possible. So here I am, sweating like a pig, nerves frayed.

What if they agree?

Oh hell, what if they don't? The prospect of zero debt, Taeler's college paid for by someone else, and proving to everyone I'm not worthless has filled my thoughts the last few days.

Now I'm here.

Shit, things just got real. This is happening.

The fancy décor and furniture in the large room Kyle leads me into match the opulence from the hallway. It resembles a posh living room rather than a boardroom, dotted with four large leather chairs and two dark fabric-covered couches centered around an imposing wooden table.

The four older men stand from where they sat as we enter the room. The lone woman remains seated as she types furiously on the cell phone inches from her scowling face. My eyes scan the room, falling on the mystery man from the hall. Pure hate fills his eyes from his perch against a sideboard, its top littered with decanters of various sizes and shapes, all filled to the brim with honey-colored liquid.

"My assistant and attorneys," Kyle states with a wave of his hand, not bothering with introducing everyone by name. "Sit." He points to the smaller couch. "We have significant information to discuss and little time to work with."

The delicious aroma of fresh-brewed coffee hits my nose, and a slow throb pulses in my head with the need for more caffeine. I dismiss Kyle, heading straight for the narrow buffet along the opposite wall. My mouth waters as the steaming dark brew streams from the thick metal carafe into my awaiting white mug. Wouldn't be shocked if the shit's china. Rich bastards. Even their mugs are fancier than me.

After one Splenda and a dash of cream—it's here, so why the hell not—I wrap both hands around the warm mug and turn to the group.

"Now I'm ready," I announce, sinking into the soft plush couch. The cushion molds around my ass and back like a fucking cloud.

Holy fuck, expensive furniture is soft.

Kyle sneers, gracefully sliding into the dark leather chair opposite me.

"After running the numbers and taking preliminary surveys, we found that, as far-fetched as it seems, you becoming running mate in next year's election will elevate the ticket higher in the polls." The white mug slips in my tight grip. "We need to switch the names on the paperwork as soon as possible. The convention is right around the corner, and all delegates must announce their candidacy by that time."

Little waves ripple along the surface of my coffee, my hands trembling in anticipation. I lift it to my lips, take a scalding sip, and then lean forward, setting it on the table.

Should I find a coaster or something?

I swipe both damp palms down my gray slacks. "Great, so what do you need from me? Birth certificate and proof of residency are two that come to mind that are required for eligibility."

An older, balding man slides a manila folder across the table. "We need several items to complete the submission process." I stop its path before it tips to the floor. "The list is in there, along with several forms that you must sign."

"Great." *Not great. So not great right now. Maybe it's not too late to back out. What the hell was I thinking! I can't do this, help run a fucking country. Maybe if I avoid eye contact and make a break for the exit, they'll forget I was ever here.*

"I asked my attorneys to draw up an agreement detailing everything we discussed. That is also in there," Kyle says, nodding to the folder in my hands.

My eyes flick to the door. If I back out now, what is there to go home to?

Just breathe, Randi. Deep inhale and slow exhale.

"Moving on to your cover story."

My brows draw together. "Cover story? I thought you wanted me *because* of my background, not despite it."

He nods, steepling two fingers beneath his dimpled chin. "With you switching from my wife to filling the vice president slot, we only need select portions of your background known, not everything."

"I don't understand." I shake my head and glance around the room, hoping someone will fill in the missing pieces.

"He means they need you poor, but not the poor white trash you are."

"Fuck you," I grit out to the man smirking against the sideboard. Knew he was an asshole the moment I laid eyes on him in the hallway. "Who the hell are you, anyway?"

"Shawn Whit," Kyle says with a tight smile. "Shawn's blunt but correct. We've decided to embellish your backstory so it's not so fucking depressing. No one would believe some low-rent trailer trash would be effective in the VP seat."

I relax, sinking farther into the seat. I'm not mad—I'm relieved. The thought of the whole world knowing everything added more pressure to the already crushing weight resting on my shoulders.

"I can see that angle. What are you suggesting we change?"

"We keep your loser mother out of the press. Instead we give the media a softer version of your story, a version we can spin to appeal to the voters."

"Sounds like a back-ass way of saying you want to lie to the voters."

No surprise that he ignores the accurate comment. "It will take a lot of maneuvering inducements—"

"Bribes. It's called a bribe, which is illegal," I interject.

"—but we'll make sure only the parts we want of your backstory make it to the press. If we feed them the information, they'll never bother digging to verify the facts."

"Now *that* I believe," I mutter. Leaning forward, I grasp the warm mug and take a long drink. I savor the warmth the liquid ignites down my throat, the smooth flavor unlike anything I've ever had. Bet it's laced with diamond dust or gold flecks. "I don't think it'll work, but you're the one in charge of this evil plot."

"I'll get the basic points of your improved background that you'll need to memorize before we hit the campaign trail. Also, to keep the media busy, the campaign will lead the press to believe we're romantically involved. Those idiots thrive on a good love story, a rags-to-riches sob story. Plus, it will give you a small foothold in the DC social scene if you're linked to me and my family name. If they think we're together maybe a few key circles will accept you, but it's a long shot. Now the next step, making you look the part."

I sink deep into the soft cushion, hoping it can swallow me whole. Every eye in the room zeros in, scanning me from head to toe, scrutinizing very inch.

"Hair, obviously," says the woman. For the first time since I entered the room, her attention focuses on me instead of the phone glued to her hands. "A few chemical peels can improve her skin tone." *Yikes. Didn't realize it was that bad.* "Botox around the forehead and eyes to make her appear less worn." I'd be pissed if I didn't agree with her assessment. "Lip injections, fast-track Invisalign, plus several whitening treatments."

Hell, maybe Ben is right. I am haggard. All that sounds not only expensive but painful. Not that they would have any sympathy to my plight.

"Is there enough time to make her believable?" Kyle asks. He leans back in the chair, blue eyes still assessing. "We only have two months until the convention."

The woman's blonde hair swishes along her collarbone. Everything about her is perfectly placed. Not a single wrinkle mars her crisp suit, and her makeup is dewy in all the right places, giving off a refreshed look. Unease rolls in my gut. I shift my focus from her to the table, unable to take her disapproving scowl any longer.

"It won't be perfect, though a vast improvement from the distressed appearance she has now. We can continue the various treatments through the campaign as well. At that point the changes will be gradual. No one will take notice."

"Add in some etiquette classes." Shawn smirks. "I bet she eats with her fucking toes."

My nose and lips tug in a sneer. The earlier embarrassment vaporizes, red-hot anger blasting through my veins instead. "Fuck you." Palms pressed to the leather, I pitch forward, ready to tackle the asshole.

Shawn chuckles, glass clicking along the sideboard as he stands from his perch on the edge. "You've said that already. If you keep it up, I'll take you up on it. After the improvements, obviously."

"Great. So that settles it." Kyle's fingers dig into the cushioned arms of the chair. Standing, he straightens his navy pin-striped suit coat. "Shawn will be our advisor through the campaign." He gestures to the narcissist whose death I'm already mentally plotting. "What he says goes, just the same as me. You will do everything we tell you, or this contract will not only be voided, preventing any future payments from the Birmingham trust, but we will also pursue legal action against you, demanding repayment of every cent we've paid out to that point."

The blood drains from my face. "What?" I gasp.

"This guarantees your cooperation," Kyle says with a haughty chuckle. "We hold the cards, not you. Get used to it and maybe you'll survive this with minimal damage."

My mouth gapes, my coffee forgotten between my hands, as Kyle, the woman, and the four men file out of the room.

Nausea rolls as fear coils in my gut. Real fear. I've had tough times, had to get myself out of difficult situations, but this is different. I'm in over my head, *way* over my head, with no one on my side. These men are ruthless. I suspected this town is run by men like this, but when the evil and manipulation stare you in the eye, ripping through your soul, it's like a backhand to the face.

"Hey, Trailer." Slowly I lift my unfocused gaze to Shawn. Shoulder against the doorframe, dark eyes glinting in the overhead lights, the evil rolls off him, filling the room. "You're mine, puppet. Let the fun begin."

CHAPTER FIVE

TREY

JANUARY

"It's open," I shout over my shoulder, eyes glued to the live debate on TV. Heavy footsteps thump closer as the person moves from the front door deeper into my condo. Tipping the near-empty beer bottle back, I flick my gaze to Tank as he falls into one of the five leather recliners stationed around the TV.

"Game's on," he grunts as he rearranges in an attempt to sink deeper into the soft leather. "Why are you watching this shit?"

Hitting the Mute button, I keep my eyes on the screen.

"Can you believe this?" I point the remote at the television, where a man and woman debate back and forth. "This candidate and the bullshit platform she's taking. No doubt she's lying through her perfect teeth, and the general public is fucking buying it. People are idiots if they believe someone like her is any different than the rest of the corrupt fucks running for office."

"Then turn it off." Tank's eyes slide shut. "When's the food getting here? I'm fucking starving."

"Second dinner?"

"Damn straight," he grunts. "That health crap Sarah forces us to eat isn't enough. Look at me." He waves up and down his massive body. "This tank don't run on fucking kale. I swear that woman's trying to kill me. I love my wife, but damn, give me the meats."

I smirk and shake my head. With a groan of my own, I shove from the recliner and amble to the kitchen. Head deep in the fridge, I shout, "That wife of yours is deadly in her own right; she doesn't need to kill you by starvation." The door rattles, beer bottles clanking together. I pinch my lips, letting out a short, high-pitched whistle. "You want a beer?"

A deep chuckle vibrates through the condo. "Hell no." He lifts his tight T-shirt up his chest, displaying the rippled six-pack he's so proud of. "With a body like this, I don't waste calories on beer."

I pop the cap on the bottle and toss it into the trash. I'm not worried about my figure. No one's warming my bed at night; no need to put in the hours at the gym to stay chiseled. The cold white marble digs into my side as I lean against it. "I know you're just saving those precious calories for your other addiction."

The man is the purest definition of a badass, yet he has a soft spot for one delicious treat.

Chocolate.

What can I say? My best friend has many strange quirks; that's just one of many. Not that I can judge, since I have plenty of my own. We balance each other. He's calm to my knee-jerk reactions. I'm the crazy offsetting his boring ass. At the academy we hated each other, mostly due to our equally fierce competitive spirits. We both strived to be first in everything, but in the end, we recognized we were more successful as a team rather than fighting each other. He's been my best friend ever since. The only real, honest man in this damn city.

I turn my attention back to the debate. My eyes narrow at the woman on the screen. She's beautiful, no doubt about that. Everything about her is perfect, from her dark, silky, full hair to the flawless makeup and St. John's suit. It's not her perfection I don't like, it's her type. The woman on the screen is the same as every other woman in this city. Beautiful, smart, the perfect arm candy for an up-and-coming politician. I know her kind—Mom. Fucked her kind—way too many to name. Fell for her kind—She Who Must Not Be Named. I'm over it. Over them, their agendas, the backstabbing and manipulating. Done.

This is my life, and I will live it the way I want, no matter the consequences.

"What's up your ass?" Tank questions. "You look like you have gas or something."

I loosen my lips softening the snarl and roll my shoulders to drop them from my ears.

"Her. I've known enough of her kind. No way in hell can I be around someone like that all day every day. What will we do if they win the primary and we're on her protection detail? Can you imagine the fucking drama that surrounds someone like her?"

"Our job doesn't change just because she's a woman. Makes it a little more challenging, but it's still a job nonetheless. It wouldn't be a problem if we were still on the VP's alpha team."

"That old fuckstick was asking for it and you know it." Of course he's still stuck on my fuckup from last year. I've gotten over it, somewhat. It's been a fun vacation, if you enjoy zero true responsibility and daily paper shuffling.

Who am I kidding? It's terrible. These past several months sitting idle have turned me bitter.

Didn't life used to be fun? Fun was before the demotion, before I realized Rachel was using me, before Mom and Dad threw down their ultimatum.

I point the lip of the bottle to the TV. "I'll bet you a hundred dollars that woman is a complete fraud, and this scheme she and Birmingham are spinning will fall apart."

"I'll take that bet. I doubt she's what you're thinking."

I scoff. Sliding onto the barstool, I lean back against the counter and stretch my arms along the top. "Look at her. No way that woman grew up the way she's saying. Lower middle class, my ass. For fuck's sake, she went to Harvard. I've never met anyone who wasn't a trust fund baby who went there."

"You're one to talk about trust fund babies," he grumbles under his breath.

"They haven't shown anything about this small town she says she's from. Nothing on her background, period. I'm telling you it's all made up to be some sob story. And don't get me going on her and that fucktard Birmingham. Of course they're a couple." My grip tightens, the sweaty bottle slipping in my palm. "Women like her are the same. Power-hungry users. All of them."

"Wow." Shoving from the chair, Tank lumbers over and leans a stocky hip against the counter. "You're one jaded son of a bitch, you know that? Not all women are like—"

"Don't even think about saying her name." It's bad enough I thought it. I shove the rising anger and regret back into the dark cavern where it belongs.

He raises both hands in surrender. "All I'm saying is you're being fucking judgmental right now. You don't know shit about that woman."

"I know enough," I say with a wave of my hand to the TV. "Every news channel is practically screaming that those two are a couple. And considering I've never heard of this Randi Sawyer until recently, I'm going with they're in it together. Just another power couple in the making."

"You can't be serious. Ever heard of the term 'fake news'?"

"This is different."

Tank chuckles. "Right." His back straightens, going on high alert at the shrill of my phone.

"That'll be the food." I swipe the screen and press a button, buzzing the kid up. "And listen, I'm not anti-women. I'm just… anti-that." I say with a nod to the screen. "Someone who will be whatever pawn they need to be to get ahead. And considering I've been up close and personal with women like that my whole life, I know what to look for. That woman is a fucking puppet if I've ever seen one. Look at her. No one looks that good unless they've grown up with money."

A knock on the door stops my rant. Grumbling under my breath I stride to the door and yank it open.

"Mr. Benson," the freckle-faced kid squeaks. "Your order from Uncle Wong's." Focusing on the receipt, he recites, "A number seven, number six with extra sauce, number three, two number tens, and an order of fried rice."

I nod, digging into the pocket of my black gym shorts. The kid's eyes widen at the hundred-dollar bill I slap in his extended hand. Generous, sure, but it's the smallest bill I have on me.

"Keep the change, kid." I slide the white plastic bags off his arm, tip my head in a silent goodbye, and let the door shut behind me.

A roaring crowd greets my ears over the rustle of plastic as I organize the various Styrofoam to-go containers along the bar. I swipe my tongue along my lower lip, eyeing the food to choose which to start with. I quickly snag the number three box. My muscles pull and ache as I stretch over the bar, dipping my hand low to reach into the drawer that holds my favorite set of porcelain chopsticks.

Positioning the two together, I shovel three pieces of sauce-covered chicken into my mouth before attempting to chew.

"I think you're wrong."

I raise my brows in Tank's direction. "Rarely. But what am I wrong about?"

"About that Randi woman. I think you're wrong. There's something about her, the way she carries herself. I think that's what you're seeing that you think is fake. It's not her background she's faking; it's the person she's trying to be for the DC dipshits."

I stare at my friend, lost for words. Maybe he's right. Doubt it, but maybe. Only time will tell, and it doesn't make any difference if she doesn't win.

"I'm surprised you don't love her for kicking that weasel Shawn Whit off Birmingham's ticket."

A barely chewed piece of chicken lodges in my throat. Coughing, I pound a fist against my chest to dislodge the bit of food. "What?" I croak out.

Tank's dark eyes glide from the TV to meet my own. "You didn't know that little tidbit? Rumor has it your favorite girlfriend stealer was the original choice for Birmingham's VP pick, not that Randi lady. Right before they had to file their registration, boom, it's her name instead of Shawn's. Interesting, right?"

"Very," I say after chugging half the beer to clear my throat. "Wonder what that's about."

Tank shrugs. "See, you don't know everything. Don't go tossing out judgments until you hear it from the source is all I'm saying."

Shawn is as manipulative and underhanded as they come in DC. I would know since we practically grew up together.

I shake off the shiver of apprehension that bolts down my spine. If that Randi Sawyer did knock Shawn off the ticket, she better watch her back. That man will be out for blood if they win. For her sake, I hope it's not true. I know firsthand the joy Shawn gains from watching other people suffer due to his actions. Borderline sociopath if you ask me.

I stare at the congealed sauce at the bottom of the container. Maybe Tank's right. Maybe I am jaded. I'm just over this city and the phonies in it. Everyone doing whatever they can to get ahead. Using, manipulating, lying—nothing is off the table.

After everything I've seen growing up in this fake-ass political circus, how could I not be jaded? This past year hasn't been a breeze either. Is this a good way to live, this bitter version of myself? No, but if I keep my guard up, no one will make me a fool again.

"Yeah," I mutter. Turning, I gaze out the wall of floor-to-ceiling windows, marveling at the soft glow of the Capitol Building. "Doubtful, but maybe. Let's just hope they don't win."

"I've heard she had a few run-ins with protesters. The campaign hired additional security for her."

"Wonder why?" I muse before shoving a warm dumpling into my open mouth.

Eyes glued to the game, Tank shrugs. "No idea. Maybe some people don't like the idea of a woman potentially being in the VP spot, or they don't like the idea of someone outside of the political powerhouse families in the election at all. All I'm saying is if they do get the nod for their party, it could get ugly early."

"Well, that could be fun. Change of pace."

"Fun for who?" He chuckles.

"Us, of course. Even before the demotion, the prior years were boring as shit. Why else do you think I stirred up so much trouble?"

"If I'd known that, I would've given you more to do," Tank mutters under his breath as he strides across the living room, eyes on the food.

"You love me and the entertainment I bring to the table."

He snatches the disposable set of chopsticks I launch at his head right before they smack his face. "Tell yourself whatever you need to make you feel loved."

"That hurts, man," I say with my lips around the top of the beer bottle. I tip it back only to get a few drops of backwash. Disgusting.

"The truth hurts. Speaking of your desperate longing for someone to love you, how are your parents?"

He should be glad I'm not carrying right now. Fucking prick.

"Still disappointed in my life choices and making sure I'm aware of that fact every time I see them. Last week my mom pulled me aside and asked me when I'm going to grow up and get a real job."

"Wow," Tank says around a mouthful of food. "Man, this is good."

I slide off the stool and make my way to the fridge. "Yep. They had the perfect plan for my life before I went and destroyed it. If I'd stayed true to their timeline, I'd be the one running for the president gig, not Birmingham." Swiping a bottle of water and another beer from the fridge, I kick it closed behind me. "His name being all over the news is making it worse. They can't stand that family, even though they're best friends. I know it's killing Mom and Dad both that Kyle is the political poster child, not me."

The stool wobbles on the tile as I sit back down, placing the bottle of water in front of Tank. Lifting the hem of my T-shirt, I wrap my hand in it and twist the cap off the beer.

"Knowing you all these years, I can't imagine you shoved into one of those political figure roles. You'd be like a bull in a china shop."

No doubt. It's why I went into the army after college. Damn, my parents were pissed when they learned I'd signed up without telling them. It pissed them off even more when not even their name—or their money—could change my enlistment. Best decision I ever made, breaking free from their perfect plan. There isn't a doubt in my mind that I would be as miserable as they are if I hadn't.

Not that the past year has been that great, but the others have. And the ones after this one will be. Change is coming; I can almost feel it. The past few weeks, I've been antsy, tense, like I'm waiting for something.

But *what* is the question.

CHAPTER SIX

RANDI

Holding in a shallow breath, I tug back the gold and green embellished curtain, peeking into the ballroom.

Wall-to-wall people dressed to the nines fill the room all laughing and mingling with a thrill of excitement in the air.

After various live debates and the hundreds of speaking engagements throughout the campaign, I'm used to all this. Well, except the pointed, hateful glares from those who deem me unworthy. No matter how many pep talks I give myself in the mirror, those crush the part of me that wants to be accepted.

They don't know me. They think they do because of what our campaign has told them, but they don't. No one out in the crowd knows the person they see in front of them night after night isn't the real Randi Sawyer. No, the real me was polished, waxed, highlighted, and sculpted away. Am I the perfect Politician Barbie? Yes. But not really me.

Not that I miss the five-dollar box dye job or the scratchy second-hand clothes, but I *do* miss having a choice in what I wear and say. For a chance at being more than the trailer park stigma, I gave up control of my life. Now here I am, about to walk on stage with Politician Ken to celebrate our primary win.

Now on to the general election.

I shake my head, dispelling the list that needs to be done and checked off for the next stage of the campaign trail. That prep can wait till tomorrow, because tonight I celebrate this win. In November, my name, Randi fucking Sawyer, will be listed as Kyle Birmingham's running mate on the presidential ballot for the United States of America.

Fucking hell.

Shit, hope I didn't say that out loud.

I cut my eyes left and then right just to be sure I'm alone in case another foul word slips. Per my etiquette teacher, cussing is trashy and unladylike. It was one of the first things they 'cured' me off. Like I had some kind of disease or something. But they can't control my inner thoughts—hell, I can't even control them. That's where I win in the long run. I'm the picture-perfect candidate for Kyle and Shawn, but inside, I'm holding tight to the pieces they're trying to erase. The pieces that make me, me.

I shift from one black stiletto to the other as I take one last look over the crowd. Over a thousand people wait to hear us, but not a single one I know. Taeler wasn't invited, by me, in a precise power move to keep her away from these leeches. The farther she is from this town, away from this corruption, the better.

I smirk.

Shit.

Fuck.

Damn.

Ha, they can't control me. In my head, I imagine raising a fist and shaking it in the air with my middle finger proudly extended. I glance over one shoulder, then the other, and my smile falters. The area surrounding me is vacant, signaling once again that I'm in this alone. Not even a single somewhat friend to laugh with about my crazy imagination.

I let out a slow, resigned sigh and release the curtain, the edge floating back into place.

"We're almost up, Walmart," Kyle says behind me.

I nod and turn back toward the stage to wait for the signal to walk out.

I gasp in a lungful of cologne filled air when something wraps around my waist. Before I can process what's happening, the heels of my stilettos teeter as I'm jerked backward, back slamming against Kyle's hard chest.

"We should properly celebrate after the party, together," he whispers against the shell of my ear.

I cough at the overwhelming smell of his cologne. *Damn, does he bathe in the shit?* "Not a chance," I grit out, shoving his arm down to release his hold on my waist. "Now let me go, you fucking bastard."

I grunt, a puff of air pushing past my lips as he adds pressure around my ribs. I gulp down tiny breaths, desperate for more than his tightening arm allows.

"All those etiquette classes and still that trash mouth of yours." Nose against the sensitive skin of my neck, he inhales. A shiver of disgust racks my shoulders. "You feel this between us. I know you do. We can be enemies and lovers too."

"You're delusional." Desperation shoots through my core, turning my movements frantic. I already dislike touch. Add in this scenario.... Tears, as well as panic, set in. "Let go, Kyle."

"Hmm, I don't think so." He chuckles into my hair. "Keep wiggling that fine ass of yours against my dick, Walmart, and I might not wait until after the party."

I still, the rapid rise and fall of my chest my body's only movement. My eyes dart around the dark backstage area, desperate to locate anyone who will stop this. Movement toward the back corner catches my attention. Locking eyes with the woman with a clipboard in her hands, I open my mouth to beg for help but snap it shut at the shake of her head. A single tear streaks down my cheek as I watch her walk away, leaving me alone with Kyle once again.

"You're acting like you have a choice in this, Walmart." The room spins, my brain barely able to keep up with the quick movement. The buttons of his dress shirt press against the exposed skin of my chest. "It's not a matter of if, but when." Hot breath brushes over my damp cheek. "You're a fool if you think you're anything more than a pawn in our game. I *own* you. I own you, your family, your whole fucking life. Every dollar I've paid wasn't a damn charity. It's a debt. One I will collect on one day soon."

Focusing the building fear into panicked strength, I press both palms against his chest and shove back as hard as I can. A demented smirk spreads across his face as he eases his hold. The unexpected release sends me staggering back, barely regaining my balance before I fall to the floor.

"Now, back to business. We've gotten this far, but we still have the main election to win. And believe me, Walmart, you don't want to find out what will happen if we lose." His cold eyes rake up and down my body, eyeing the curves my snug red dress accentuates. "Do whatever it takes to ensure a win in November. I don't care who you have to bribe, suck off, fuck, or kill. We have to win. It's not just your life depending on it."

My mouth gapes at the insinuation.

He wouldn't. Would he?

"Kyle." My head whips to the side as a suit-clad Shawn appears from the shadowed corner. The earlier light lunch churns in my belly at his evil smirk. "You're up."

"Right," Kyle acknowledges, shifting his hungry eyes from me with a long breath. "We're up. Let's go."

I scowl at Shawn as Kyle takes his sweet-ass time to adjust his suit jacket and smooth down his tie. A bright fake smile, one I've become very familiar with the last several months, spreads up Kyle's cheeks before he steps out onto the stage, waving.

"Why didn't you stop that?" I say, anger and confusion hardening my tone.

Shawn's smile falls. "I cannot believe someone as stupid as you took my spot on the ticket. You think I give a fuck what he does to you, Trailer? We own you from now until you lose or you're dead, and honestly, I fucking hope it's the latter. You don't deserve to be here, breathe the same air as us. I've worked my whole damn life for this shot, and you took it from me. You will pay."

The crowd behind the curtain roars in excitement at something Kyle said onstage. They're none the wiser about what's going on backstage—not that they would care or do anything to stop Shawn's threats.

My heart plummets, stomach rolling. I seal my hand over my mouth to hold back the bile rising in my throat. I shove around him and race to the bathroom. The door barely snickers shut before I vomit into the sink. My arms tremble under my weight, the white porcelain sink cool beneath my clammy palms. His words shouldn't rock me that much; the subtle threats are nothing new. The past few months he's done nothing but taunt and torture me with his words.

They know I'm trapped. *I* know I'm trapped, their caged plaything they enjoy tormenting. Everything I was promised, everything they've done to this point, adds to my gilded prison, locking me into doing their daily bidding. But tonight Kyle changed the game, stepped over the invisible line they've toed the past several months by touching me. Not that it changes anything. I'm still bound to them until this is done, and no one would care if I spoke up about their terrible treatment. Plus, it's not like my life didn't prepare me for this. At least now I'm beautifully dressed, have a sweet-ass condo, and more spending money than I can imagine in exchange for the daily torment; in the past, it came free to the bully.

I scan my reflection in the nearby mirror, carefully using the image to wipe away the smeared black mascara lines striping my cheek from the earlier tears. Shawn's threats, Kyle's advances. I have to see this through like I've done my whole life.

Prepare, plan, and push forward. This is my checklist, what will help me survive the next few months and next four years if we win. No, not if—*when* we win. I can't go back home now, a failure. No, I'll put up with their shit, and we will win.

I've accomplished everything I've set my mind to doing, and this is no different.

Graduating on time as a teen mom at the top of the class. Check.

Get into University of Texas. Check.

Score high on the LSAT for top law schools to take notice. Check.

Convince Harvard to offer me more grants and scholarships than anyone before. Check.

This is simply another hurdle in life. Win the election, no matter the cost, so Kyle doesn't kill me and hide the body, and don't let him touch me. Oh, and watch my back for when Shawn is there, eager to plunge a knife in when I'm not looking.

This would be easier if I had someone to confide in, someone to trust. But finding that someone in this town won't happen.

I'll tackle this like every other hurdle I've met in my life.

All on my own.

BEFORE THE BLACK limo's door shuts, I toe off one black Louboutin and then the other, the shoes clattering to the floorboard. An unlady-like groan pushes past my lips as I wiggle my toes in their newfound freedom. Beautiful shoes, comfortable too, until hour four of standing in them. I didn't pick them out, or the beautiful dress I'm wearing. All my outfits and clothes are coordinated by my wardrobe consultants. Who knew that's a real job.

I don't glance back as the car smoothly pulls from the curb, easing into the constant traffic. I'll get an earful tomorrow from the campaign manager for leaving early, but I don't care. The cool, soft leather seeps through the back of my dress as I lean back, inhaling deeply for the first time all night. Pressing the heels of both hands to my cheeks, I massage the ache away. Holding that wide fake smile all night burned some serious calories. Head thumping back against the headrest, I allow my eyes to close.

The edges of my lips dip as I recall the night's events. My dress was gorgeous, shoes perfection, makeup and hair flawless—and still no one paid me any attention. Not that I wanted to fake chitchat with people I don't know, but feeling like you have the plague isn't the best way to spend an evening either.

Blowing out a slow breath, I relax my tense muscles. It's irrational that in this limo, alone, the suffocating weight of loneliness is less than earlier in a room filled to the brim with people.

The revving of a car engine draws my attention out the window. I gasp, hands slapping the seat for support. Glass shatters as metal against metal screeches through the night. I sail through the air, my head smacking the opposite window. The world spins, my thoughts fuzzy.

Blinking through the pain radiating through my scalp and shoulder, I open my mouth to shout for help.

I don't get the chance.

Another impact, this time from behind, rockets me forward. A scream scratches its way up my throat, but the screeching of rubber against asphalt gobbles up the sound.

Warm liquid trickles over my upper lip, building along the seam before seeping in between.

Demanding shouts call outside the destroyed limo, barely audible over the sharp ringing in my ears. I give my head a small shake, immediately regretting the movement as pain flares unbidden. My throbbing head gripped between my palms, I give it a hard press to prevent it from exploding from the building pressure.

More glass shatters, fragments scratching down my back.

The voices grow louder. Shock takes over all rational thought. Curling into the fetal position, I cover both ears to keep them from rupturing at the blaring sounds.

What the hell is going on?

Forcing my eyes open, I blink several times. Blocks of light from the streetlights seep through the shattered windows. Shadows shift outside, their inky figures skirting across the seat and floorboard.

I hiss through clenched teeth as I move across the floorboard toward the still-intact door. Everything pulses with sharp, breath-catching pain. Shards of glass slice at my knees and palms, but still I continue toward freedom.

The putrid scent of burning rubber wafts through the destroyed passenger compartment.

"Fuck," I wheeze. Lunging for the door, I grip the handle and shove.

It doesn't budge. A stronger waft of smoke fuels my frantic attempt at escape.

I will *not* burn to death in this fucking limo. Nope. Light breaks through the darkness, the grind of metal against metal piercing my sensitive ears.

A head pops through the now-open door. "Ma'am, we need to get you out of here."

Relief swells in my chest, calming my stroke-level pulse at the authoritative male voice.

I'm getting out of here. Today is not my death day. Whew.

"No shit." Okay, apparently near-death experiences shift the real Randi back into the driver seat of my mouth.

He dips farther through the door into the tattered interior, a hint of a smirk shining on his face. "Now," he commands.

I eagerly accept his extended hand. Calluses scrape along my palm as our hands slide together.

"So bossy," I grumble. I scoot across the leather, careful to not pierce my ass with the broken window bits. At the door, he snakes an arm around my waist and hoists me into the air.

My eyes dart around, taking in the flashing lights and utter chaos. A crowd with flashing cameras shouts from behind a line of suited men while another group on the other side of the street jerks hand-made signs in the air, their faces contorted in anger.

"What... what the hell happened?" I ask, confusion filling my soft tone. He takes several long strides away from the limo with me still pressed tightly to his hard chest. "What are you're doing? I can walk."

"The glass, ma'am. You're not wearing shoes."

Okay, he has a point, but still, he could've asked.

I shift my focus from the crowds toward the direction he's headed. The bright lights of my condo building's overhang blare through the night across the block. At his back, lights continue to flash, red and blue beams like a colorful strobe light coming from the few police cars.

"Get her inside," says a deep, masculine voice. I peer over my hero's shoulder, and my eyes widen. The man is a fucking tank. The light reflects off his smooth bald head, shadows contouring to highlight his bulky frame. His dark eyes scan the area over and over again.

"Oh really," says the man holding me. "You don't say. Can't believe we let these fuckers slip through. We've gotten rusty sitting on the sidelines."

Despite the circumstances, a smile tugs at my lips.

"Not the time or place, Benson," the big guy says. "A doctor will be up in five."

"Where were those rent-a-cops she's had on her?"

"Not sure. Working on it." The big man presses two fingers to his ear. "On my way." His narrowed eyes meet mine before flicking to the man cradling me in his arms. "Just get her inside. We'll figure the rest out after we're secure."

Even with the man's quick steps, rushing us toward the glass doors of the condo lobby, his tight hold keeps me snug against his chest, preventing any jostling. Leaning back a bit to look over his shoulder, I sweep the area until I find the limo.

"What the...?" I whisper to myself as I scan the wreckage. The damage centers around the passenger compartment, the driver side unharmed except for where it nailed a light pole. "This is getting out of hand."

The man's annoyed huff pulls my gaze from the totaled limo to his face, and I take in every handsome detail. Light brown eyes rapidly scan our surroundings. Straight nose, nostrils flaring with each heavy breath. A full bottom lip presses tight against a thinner upper one, the soft pink color draining, leaving the inside edges white. Happy wrinkles crease his cheeks and the edges of his eyes from years of smiling. Naturally unblemished tan skin and silky, dark chocolate floppy hair accentuate his overall appeal. Attractive in a happy, mischievous way.

I lower my scrutinizing gaze to a dress shirt, tie, and suit jacket.

All the pieces snap together.

Of course they're Secret Service. I'm grateful for their presence tonight, but now that they're here, it means they're here to stay until the general election in November. Two whole months. I begged the previous security detail to keep their distance, allowing some semblance of privacy. There's no way I'll convince these guys of the same. They're hard core.

Those honey brown eyes pause their scan to meet mine.

I attempt a convincing smile, but a sharp pain slices through my head, turning it into a grimace.

"Knew you'd be full of drama," he mutters under his breath, which happens to be by my ear, as we step through an open door into the lobby. "You politicians will do anything for publicity."

Seriously? Him fucking too?

I'm so damn tired of people thinking they know me based on what they see. I thought being here, looking like this, changing my background would make people see me as an equal. But instead it's another set of judgments, different stigma for people to assume.

How do I change someone's perspective if they assume who I am instead of learning for themselves? If people continue to tell me who I am based on what they see, why should I keep fighting to prove them wrong?

CHAPTER SEVEN

RANDI

"I said I'm fine," I say with a sigh as the doctor sticks a metal contraption inside my ears. "My head hurts, my palms sting from the cuts, but that's it."

"You're not fine," the woman says again. The same words have been exchanged several times over the past hour. "Considering I'm the one with a medical degree in this room, we'll stick with *my* assessment over yours."

"Whatever," I grumble and lie back on the soft bedding, my legs dangling over the end. I nibble on the bright red-painted nail of my middle finger.

On the other side of the bedroom door, distorted male voices draw my attention. No one has mentioned anything regarding the wreck, which is fucking irritating. Add in my pounding head, which Miss 'I'm right because I have a medical degree' diagnosed as a mild concussion, and I'm on the sharp edge between holding it together and losing my ever-loving shit.

"Someone will need to wake you up every few hours tonight," the woman says more to the tablet in her hand than me. "Do you have someone?"

"No, it's just me."

Her gaze slowly rises from the screen, brow arched. "What about Mr. Birmingham? When will he be by?"

Fire ignites my blood, and I harden my features, narrowing my eyes into menacing glare. "He won't come by because he doesn't live here."

"Sorry, I just assumed...."

Of course that's what she assumed since the media has spewed tidbits about our fake relationship across every news channel. This is the part I hate the most about the lies we leaked to the press.

"Your assumption is wrong." Elbow digging into the duvet, I push myself up. I squint as the doctor splits, morphing into two people. "Doc, did you happen to clone yourself in the last two seconds?"

Both doctors frown. "Upgrading that concussion to severe."

When the two doctors mold back into one, I sit up straight on the bed. "When will someone update me on tonight?"

"As soon as we're done."

I flick my gaze to the closed door. "Then we're done. Leave a list of what I need to do tonight for the concussion, and I'll set my alarm."

"You really need someone to—"

"Well, lady," I say, pushing off the bed to stand. Tightening the sash of my long-sleeve terry cloth robe, I step toward the door. "I'm used to doing this thing called life on my own, so I'll figure it out." At the door, I turn the brass knob and pull it open. I wave a hand through the air, gesturing out the door with a smile. "Thank you for your help tonight. Contact my admin for payment." Because on top of the wardrobe coordinators, I also employ an admin to handle bills, flights, personal errands, and who knows what else.

With a huff, she storms out of the room. Without looking into the craziness of the living room, I slam the door shut behind the doctor and lean against it. A few bruises, cuts, and a concussion aren't too bad considering my end of the limo was crushed.

I chew on a manicured nail as I shuffle toward the en suite bathroom. For an additional layer of protection against... everyone, I lock the bathroom door behind me. The marble vanity digs against my lower belly as I lean closer to the mirror, inspecting the wounds for myself.

I tilt my head one way and then the other. The image follows. It's me—I'm not that crazy—but the woman staring back at me doesn't look like me.

The woman in the mirror strongly resembles a brunette Lindsay Lohan mug shot after an all-night bender.

Not good.

I tilt my chin down, hoping for a better angle.

Nope. Zero good angles.

I slide the multiple temporary extensions from my hair and lay them carefully on the sink. I stroke each piece, smoothing it out before pulling another free. With the final section out, I ruffle my real hair and sigh in relief. They make my hair full and beautiful but hurt after a full day of wearing so many.

Soap bubbles collect around the drain as I remove the grime from the wreck and a thousand handshakes from my hands. Pressing closer to the mirror, I widen one eye and then the other, removing the green-tinted contacts. It's nice not having to wear glasses, but the color enhancement to change my hazel to brilliant green is overboard if you ask me.

Not that anyone did.

Oh no, not once was I consulted on any of these 'enhancements.' Most days I don't recognize the beautiful woman staring back at me in the mirror. After several somewhat painful laser treatments, brown spots from years of sun damage and bad skin vanished. A little bit of lip plump here, some Botox there, a billion chemical peels, and months of Invisalign later, I'm this. Beautiful by some people's standards, a far cry from the haggard look I started with. The woman in the mirror would've been a part of the popular crowd in high school, not the weird one who ended up getting pregnant in the back seat of her boyfriend's parents' van.

Do I miss basic Randi 1.0? Yes and no. I enjoy feeling beautiful and the new attention from men, but with Randi 2.0 comes obligations and strings attached. All this and still it's not enough to be accepted in this city or back home, where people are waiting for me to fail.

Ugh. I rest my elbow on the vanity and cover my face with both hands to stop me from staring at my reflection. The condo, the makeover, the money—all for a chance to prove myself.

The intense throb in my head distracts me from the deep life thoughts I was falling into. I wince with each step to the shower. The large glass door whooshes open with a soft tug. Stretching, I twist the handle all the way right to steaming hot. Slow fingers release the sash knot and the robe parts, exposing me to the empty bathroom. I hiss through the soreness as I lift both shoulders, shrugging the soft material to pool on the heated tile floor. Initial pelts of steaming spray against the multitude of thin cuts cause bites of stinging pain along my battered skin.

I lean back, the cool tile sending a chill down my spine. A wave of homesickness barrels through me from the contradicting temperatures of the water and tile, the battle of the two similar to warm Texas spring days soaked in a cold rain shower.

Alone in the quiet, the steam wrapped around me like a security blanket, I replay the scene from earlier. Bile rises, pushing up my throat. My head screams as I pitch forward, palms slapping the opposite wall for support, and puke up the miniature hors d'oeuvres from the party.

Fuck, what will I do? Can I really expect to avoid being alone with Kyle for the next few months—or worse, four years if we win? There must be something to protect myself, but what? I'm weak. I'll own up to that. These narrow hips and soft arms didn't get their 'character' by hitting the gym, that's for sure.

I need a plan.

And mace.

Perhaps a stun gun too. Shooting those cords and electrifying Kyle's balls seems like a decent quid pro quo after his manhandling tonight. Eyes to the ceiling, I chant the words 'mace' and 'stun gun' three times to commit them to memory. This way I'll remember to add both to the Amazon cart after this glorious shower.

A sharp knock at the door sounds as I'm still weapons planning. With the pad of my thumb, I clear two small circles in the fogged glass door to clearly see through.

The door opens an inch or two, but no one steps through.

"Ma'am," a male voice calls out. "Everything okay in there?"

"Checking to make sure I cleaned behind the ears? Didn't realize that was in your job description," I mutter just loud enough for the guy on the other side of the door to hear.

"The doctor said we needed to check on you every hour."

I roll my eyes before sticking my hair under the water. "Okay, now she's just trying to piss me off. She told me every couple of hours." I attack my thick dark hair with ferocity, making layers and layers of cherry almond scented suds build along my scalp and cascade down my back. "But as you can see, or hear rather, I'm fine. Just trying to get the stench of almost-death off me."

"Ma'am?"

"What happened tonight?"

If we were in Texas, crickets would chirp in the blatant silence.

"Also, your daughter is on the phone, saying she won't hang up until she talks to you."

"What?" I growl and slam my palm against the faucet handle, cutting off the stream of water. "Why didn't you start with that?" Channeling all my anger into my movements, I snatch a towel off the nearby hook and scrub at the streams of water cascading down my body. Towel wrapped around my chest, I pause. "Wait, why did she call you?"

"She didn't, ma'am. She called your cell phone several times. By the twentieth or so missed call, we answered."

"That could've been China calling!" I yell. Okay, maybe I see how Ben believes Taeler inherited her dramatics from me.

The man on the other side of the cracked door clears his throat. "Her name was on the caller ID, and a picture of you two flashed on the screen as well, ma'am."

Hmm. Didn't think about that one.

"Good point. Still could've been China. They're sneaky little bastards. Or someone calling to tell me I was left a million dollars by a distant relative and I need to send them my social and bank account information." I chuckle to myself. I really am hilarious. Too bad either no one is around to hear me or doesn't get the brilliance of my jokes.

"I would advise against that, ma'am. Sounds fishy."

"No shit, Sherlock," I mumble under my breath as I press the length of my hair between a dry towel to remove excess water. Once again donned in the robe from earlier, I swipe my thick-frame glasses off the counter and yank the door open.

I eye the young man I've been talking to. His eyes flick from mine to the door leading to the living room and back again.

"Are you a super genius or something?" I ask, head cocked to the side as my eyes scan his baby face.

The boy's light blond brows furrow. "Ma'am?"

"How old are you? I'm guessing twenty. Did you just graduate from Secret Service school or something?" Not that I want these guys hanging around every second, but if I have to endure them, I'd prefer guys who are old enough to need a shave once a week.

Pops of crimson dot his cheeks as he shifts from one foot to the other, avoiding eye contact.

Well hell. I've embarrassed him. Sweet kid.

I hold out a hand, awkwardly patting his shoulder. "Sorry, that was rude. You're old enough, and cute." I leave off 'I could be your mom.'

"Now this I'm surprised about."

Junior and I turn to the voice on the other side of the room. I scowl at the man I recognize leaning against the far wall. He's the one who pulled me out of the town car and carried me inside. Damn, he's hot. Earlier, with my fuzzy vision and shock, I thought he was attractive, but here in my room? Attractive doesn't even count. On a scale of one to ten, he's a nine working his way to an eleven if he can grow a quick man bun. And old, thank goodness, unlike Junior here. Shit, not old. He's like my age.

"I'm not old, dammit," I mutter.

The two men exchange a quick look.

"Ma'am?" Junior asks.

I wave a hand through the air, dismissing him. "Sorry, wrong conversation."

"Did I miss something?" asks the hot, annoying one. I swear his light brown eyes fucking twinkle. *Twinkle*. Is he part unicorn or something?

"What are you surprised about?" I shoot back, relenting in our sudden stare-off.

He pushes off the wall to stalk closer. Why does he have to be such an asshole? In the baking of men, can the two ingredients hot and a nice guy not mix together or something? Even with the asshole factor, I'm drawn to him. Maybe the doc's diagnosis of a concussion is legit.

"That you'd be interested in a no one like Grem here."

My lips curve upward, matching his smirk, before my eyes track back to the Grem fellow.

"Grem, as in the Grim Reaper? You kill a lot of people or something?"

Grem chokes back a cough, whereas the hot one chuckles. "Grem, as in short for Gremlin. The kid hates the water."

"Funny. Can't wait to hear that story." I hold out my hand. "Now, give me my phone, please."

Gremlin drops the phone into my palm, avoiding skin-to-skin contact. His gaze darts from the hot guy back to me before he turns on his heels.

"Thanks," I mutter to his back as he fast-walks out of the bedroom. With a deep calming breath, I lift the cell phone to my ear. "Tae?"

"Mom! What the fuck happened to you?" I pull the phone from my ear with a cringe. The doctor did mention something about loud noises doing more damage. I think. Wasn't really listening, actually.

"Taeler Lynn, do not use that fucking language with me, dammit," I bite back. College has taught her the worst manners, I fucking swear.

Movement across the room catches my eye, reminding me I'm not alone. His lips curve in a sexy, mischievous smirk that flips my insides and warms the space between my thighs. Those brown eyes shine with amusement, his fine smile lines crinkling.

I wince at Taeler's continued high-pitched rampage on the other end. He takes a step forward, smirk gone.

"Wait," My shaky voice is barely loud enough for Taeler to hear. "Calm the hell down, Tae. My head is killing me, and your yelling is making it worse. Concussions are the worst. I wouldn't recommend ever getting one."

"Sorry, Mom, I'm just—wait, what the hell? Concussion?" A slight tremble resonates in her tone. For the second time tonight, tears build, but this time they're due to her worry instead of fear. "Mom, what happened? Tell me, please. I'm worried out of my mind over here. Do I need to fly up? I'm sure I can miss classes if you need me."

A magnetic pull draws my gaze back to the agent. "No, sweetheart, you don't need to fly up here. Everything is okay. It's being handled by the Secret Service as we speak." *Wait a second.* Careful to not make any sudden movements, I ease onto the edge of the bed and lie back. "Taeler, how did you even know something happened tonight?"

Her sigh sounds through the phone. At least she's calmed down a little. "You're all over the news. Whatever happened tonight is covered on every news channel. It's a big deal, Mom. You're a big deal now. Congratulations, by the way."

"Thanks," I mutter. "I still can't believe it." Securing the phone between my ear and shoulder, I roll to my side and swipe the remote off the side table. It clatters back onto the solid wood after I hit the Power button. No need to change the channel, since I monitored the big network news channels all morning as the votes were tallied. The large flat-screen TV snaps to life. Bright flashes from other cameras disorient the image, but the entrance to my condo building is unmistakable. Black Suburbans dot the area, along with several police cars and one fire truck. The woman on the screen waves a frantic hand behind her while talking to the camera.

"Watching now," I say more to myself than Taeler. On the other end of the line, Taeler talks a thousand words a second, demanding answers and threatening to fly up here, but all I can focus on is the footage on the screen. "Listen, Tae, I love you, but I don't know what to tell you. The Secret Service is here now and I'm safe, promise. I'll call you as soon as I know something. Love you." After a teary good-bye, the line goes dead.

Eyes still glued to the TV, I say, "Fill me in. Now."

"The investigation is ongoing. We don't know what happened," the hot agent says. You'd think his words would agitate me more, but the concern with a hint of frustration in his voice is soothing. "Not a well-thought-out plan, but still, whoever did this probably thought they could scare you out of continuing on to the general election."

"Up till this point, it's been protesters, a few things tossed on stage or toward me during a rally. Nothing violent. Whoever is behind this upped their game tonight." I tear my focus from the TV and attempt a smile. "Convenient that you and your friends were already here though. Thank you. I really didn't want to die tonight."

"Agents, not friends. And we were already here prepared to receive you after the party. I talked to the team lead while you were with the doc, and it seems there was some kind of communication breakdown. We were told the security team who's been with you up till this point would hand you off here at the condo. Instead, most were dismissed earlier today, and then the final few were told they were done after the party."

"Is my concussed brain confused or does that sound fishy? Do I have to keep you? The team, that is."

"Yes, ma'am. We're here to stay."

The room goes fuzzy as my eyes struggle to maintain focus. The daunting weight of the entire night's events settles on my shoulders. Exhaustion swoops in, draining the last bit of energy reserve I have left.

"I think I need a quick nap," I murmur. The bed dips under my hands and knees as I crawl up to the top but collapse before I can slide between the sheets.

"That's not a great decision."

"Just a few minutes, Trouble," I say on a yawn. Damn, I'm tired. The past few months—hell, few years—feel like they've finally caught up with me.

"Trouble?"

I smile into the pillow at the confusion in his voice. Maybe having these guys around won't be so bad after all.

"I can see it," I say and snuggle deeper into the soft bed. "You're trouble. I just know it. But don't worry. So am I."

He mutters something I can't make out, but I don't care. Just a few minutes of sleep; then I'll be good to go.

The last thought that slips through my mind before oblivion sinks in is the hope that he's still here when I wake up.

CHAPTER EIGHT

TREY

A swirl of conflicting emotions and indecipherable thoughts floods through my mind. What in the hell happened during the last hour? My gaze wanders up and down her robed body, inspecting each inch, hoping to find the sign to help me understand her. To say I was floored when she stepped out of the bathroom earlier is an understatement. Curled on her side, the potential VP's breathing evens out, and her shoulders relax further into the mattress. During the primaries and televised debates, she seemed plastic, too perfect. But the woman lightly snoring on the bed is the definition of *real* perfection. The no makeup, wet hair, and glasses look is one most women wouldn't dare pull off even in the privacy of their own home.

But not this woman, this Randi lady.

I narrow my eyes on her relaxed face, skimming down to focus on her slightly parted plump lips.

"What in the hell do you think you're doing?" Tank whisper-yells from the doorway.

I jolt like I've been caught doing something inappropriate, and my gaze flicks to the floor. "Nothing. She fell asleep. Just monitoring her like that doc told us to."

I glance over to Tank, whose eyes are on sleeping beauty. She mutters something unintelligible and rolls to lie on her back. I look back to her, trying and failing not to notice the bare skin of her toned calves.

Tank clears his throat, dragging my attention back to him.

"You want me to take over?" he asks.

I wave a hand, declining his offer. "I'm good." Nodding to the soft armchair in the corner, I say, "I'll wake her up in an hour."

Tank's large bald head tilts to the side. Shit, I know that look.

"Odd, don't you think?" he muses. "Earlier tonight, you were complaining about this gig, and now here you are offering to watch while she sleeps."

My shoulders rise and fall in an exaggerated shrug. "Just doing my job, you nosy shit. Nothing else."

"Right." He drags out the word, making it clear he doesn't believe me. "We're in the next room piecing shit together. Let me know if you need me."

I track him until his back disappears through the door and it clicks shut behind him. Like a magnet drawn to metal, my eyes shift back to the woman on the bed. I startle when they meet her half-open hazel ones.

"You wouldn't happen to have any water on you, would you?" she whispers like every word hurts.

I nod and point to her side table. "Bottle is beside you, along with some meds the doctor approved you to take for the headache."

"Headache doesn't even begin to describe the death metal concert going on up there." A pained gasp pushes past her lips at her attempt to sit up. "Fucking hell." She groans before giving up on her water quest and lowering back to the bed. "It's like the worst hangover ever but without all the fun and poor decisions from the night before."

I open my mouth to say something sarcastic, but her wide eyes flick to mine just as a slight green tint washes over her face.

"Shit," I grumble. I race to the bathroom, my steps pounding against the soft carpet. I skid to a stop along the tile and grab the first trash can I lay my eyes on. Emerging from the bathroom, I lunge for the side of the bed just as she leans over and vomits.

"You should've left me in the damn car." Another wave of nausea causes her to curl into a tight ball as she dry heaves into the metal bin. Tears streak down her pale face, drawing attention to the light scattering of freckles that adorn the skin along her cheekbones.

All my smartass remarks—hell, even my annoyance at the woman, which has grown every day since she first appeared in DC—evaporate at her weak state. The metal of the bin digs into my fingers as I adjust my grip to hold it in one hand. With the other, I gather her long dark hair into a tight bundle at the nape of her neck to keep it away from her face.

After a few more heaves into the bin, she waves a weak hand and falls back into the pillows. Sweat glistens on her forehead, and a pain-laced grimace scrunches her features. I set the metal can beside the door to take out later and return to the bathroom to find a towel.

Her eyes are closed when I return but flutter open when I place the cool, wet washcloth along her forehead. For a minute, we stay in the cocoon of comfortable silence. Something in her eyes pounds at the thick walls I've built, telling me to reconsider my prejudgment of her. Before I fall further under her spell, I step back from the bed, snagging the bottle of water off the nightstand.

"Here." I crack the seal and hold it out over the bed.

"Thanks." The slight tremble in her hand as she reaches for the bottle doesn't go unnoticed.

What the hell am I doing? I roll my eyes at the concern and worry building in my chest, constricting my airway. She's fine, or she will be. Why the hell do I care anyway? She's the job, and she's with that fucktard Birmingham. She's just like them, all of them, and that's why I have to keep my distance. Even if she is beautiful. And somehow funny while in pain.

"Anything new about tonight?" she mumbles after a long, deep gulp from the bottle.

"Small sips or you'll get sick again. And try to sit up more." Her hazel eyes flick to mine, and a confused look lashes across her face.

"No, I haven't heard anything new. I've been in here since you passed out on me."

Her dramatic eye roll looks painful. "I didn't pass out. I rested my eyes for a few minutes. It's been a long night okay."

"Nothing like almost getting killed to ruin an evening," I say dryly.

"Right," she groans in agreement. "Not that the party was any better. What a waste of money." Turning on her side, she tucks the edges of the robe together, covering almost every inch of her legs, and snuggles deeper into the pillow. "What's up with the small food at those things? Is it not okay to eat anymore?"

"What?"

"I mean, I had to eat like a hundred balls to—"

"Balls?" I raise my dark brows in question while attempting to hold back the laugh that wants to erupt. "You ate a hundred balls? Busy night." This time I don't mask my smirk.

Her eyes narrow before widening. "Didn't expect that."

I sink into the armchair opposite the bed. "Expect what, exactly?"

"You being funny. You seem more like a jackass with a chip on his shoulder." A sly smile tugs at the corner of her lips. She knows she's testing me, and for some reason, I'm enjoying it.

"And you seem more like a power-hungry political lackey who's willing to do anything, or anyone, to get what you want."

"I'm no one's lackey," she grits out, all humor fading into resentment.

Huh, that's the part she points out. Interesting. "Sure you aren't, puppet."

"We're done here. My head hurts," she deadpans, never dropping my gaze. Shit, if her gorgeous eyes could throw daggers, I'd be dead. "Leave. Now."

The soft fabric of the chair presses into my palms as I push against the armrests to stand. After fixing my suit jacket, I tuck both hands into my pants pockets and return her hate-filled stare.

"Don't think you can fool me, sweetheart. I see right through you."

"Might want to get your eyes checked, asshat." The edge of her left lip curls up in a snarl, but even still, she's a knockout. "But it's a good thing I don't give two shits what you or any of your little buddies out there think because—"

"Everything okay in here?" Tank's deep voice booms through the room, cutting the tight tension in the air.

Eyes still locked on mine, both of us vying for dominance, she hitches her chin. "Besides my pounding head, nausea worse than morning sickness, and this jackass pissing me off, yeah, it's just sunshine and unicorns in here."

I stifle a smirk as Tank covers his laugh with a fake cough.

"Right. Um, the nausea the doc said to expect that from the concussion, but you mentioned morning sickness. Any chance you're also...."

"Also what?"

I breathe a sigh of relief when her annoyed gaze slides to Tank. Shit, that woman can hold her own.

"Pregnant, ma'am."

An undignified snort echoes through the room. I chuckle with a shake of my head in disbelief. Who in the hell is this woman?

"No, absolutely not. You have to have sex for that to happen, if you believe my seventh-grade sex ed teacher."

My eyes meet Tank's, both of us clearly confused.

"Not that it did Mary any good, am I right?" she says with another snort. "Damn, I miss sex. Even boring, handsy sex would do at this point."

"Um... uh...," Tank stammers.

I bark out a quick loud laugh as his dark skin glows with a red tint.

"Not with you, Terminator. I see that ring on your finger. It's the first thing I noticed, that and your pretty shiny head and muscles." Her mouth stretches with a wide yawn. "And not Trouble either, unless he agrees to wear a ball gag."

"The fuck?" I say on a pushed breath.

"Night night, ladies," she mutters into her pillow as her eyes close. "I'm not good at this sleepover stuff, but next time I need wine and *Golden Girls*. 'Kay? 'Kay."

The second the last word is out, her body relaxes as she passes out cold.

I shake my head, completely dumbfounded, as Tank and I exit the room. We leave the door open a sliver to make sure we can hear her if she wakes up again.

"What in the ever-loving hell was that?" Tank asks, eyes wide in shock. "I couldn't keep up with the conversation, could you?"

"Barely. Did she call us ladies and say we were having a sleepover?" The wall shudders when my back slams against it. I pinch the bridge of my nose in an attempt to ease the pressure building behind my eyes. "How in the hell is she potentially our next VP?"

"She called me Terminator." A hint of awe clouds his tone, making me look across the room to where he's perched on a barstool.

The rest of the team ignores us as they type away on laptops and phones. I survey the room. Gremlin is nowhere to be found. Must be stationed in the hall.

"What was that about needing sex?" That gets the guys' attention. The low murmur and clicking of keys from earlier halt.

"Is there a signup sheet?" Champ offers from where he sits on the floor, laptop balanced on his knees. "I don't care if she is his sloppy seconds."

A collective growl vibrates through the room at the mention of him. No one except Shawn is more conniving, degrading, and overall a fucking bastard than Kyle Birmingham.

"No signup sheet," Tank barks. All humor melts from the room. "She hit her head, probably had no idea what in the hell she was saying. It's business as usual for us. We learn as much as we can about the attack tonight, and we do our job. You will respect her, you will protect her, and you will treat her like every other man that has come before her. Nothing changes. Got it?"

A resounding "Yes, sir" rumbles through the small room.

A drop of guilt settles in my gut. No way in hell is this business as usual. I will respect her, I will protect her, but treat her like every old fart who's been under our protection? Not a chance. First of all, I never had to deep breathe to stay focused on the job instead of their legs or had the urge to verbally spar with one just to hear what they'd say next.

No, this time it's different.

Hell, maybe I'm even different.

Maybe—

The door flies open, slamming against the wall and cutting off my thoughts. Tension consumes the room as Birmingham steps over the threshold. His cold eyes sweep across the team before settling on me. A condescending smirk rises up his prick face.

"Didn't see you with your parents tonight at the party."

I shrug, faking casualness when all I really want is to punch the slimy smirk off his Botoxed face. "Working."

"Ah, that's right. Sometimes I forget where you landed after you couldn't take the pressure of the game."

"Whatever you want to tell yourself, asshole."

The entire team snickers. I watch with pure joy and fascination as the tips of Kyle's ears redden.

"Show some respect, or I'll try you for treason after I win," he seethes. "Or maybe I'll torture you with the entertaining sex tapes Shawn and—"

Without thinking of the consequences, I lunge. Two anaconda arms wrap around my chest, hauling me backward before my swing can connect.

Rage burns through my veins, igniting my skin. With an arrogant laugh, he saunters to the bedroom door. Hand on the knob, he turns back to face me, his features hardening to stone.

"I've fucked that tight pussy so many times my dick is imprinted in her cunt. She's mine, so don't even think about touching my new favorite toy."

Fists at my side, I clench them tight and seal my lips to keep from responding.

"Good boy. And they say old dogs can't learn new tricks." He shoves the door open and steps into the bedroom.

Staring at the now closed door, I inhale a deep breath, mentally erasing every fucking emotion that woman conjured in me tonight. I erase the idea of thinking she's different than every woman I've ever met. A fucking liar. I should've known.

Turning, I yank open the front door. Gripping Gremlin's collar, I pull him into the condo and slam the door shut, leaving me alone in the hallway. Hands on my knees, I take several deep breaths, evening out my pulse and diminishing the boiling anger.

But hours later the bitter taste of disappointment hasn't faded.

CHAPTER NINE

RANDI

A cold, fear-laced shiver pulls me from a light sleep. Eyes closed, I wrap both arms around my chest to fend off the uneasy energy that's settled over my room. Something icy wraps around my ankle, slowly sliding my heel across the duvet, putting distance between it and the other. Behind my closed lids, my eyes twitch. The steady pulse in my head makes it impossible to gather enough energy to open my eyes.

"Get up, Walmart," a familiar deep voice says, cutting the ties the darkness had over me.

With a gasp, I bolt upright, eyes frantically searching the room before settling on Kyle at the end of the bed, one hand around my left ankle while he brushes his fingertips up and down my bare calf with the other. Another fear-filled shiver rattles through my body, shaking my shoulders and sending flairs of pain into my brain.

"Kyle," I rasp. Damn, my throat fucking hurts. Without taking my eyes off the pervert, I grapple for the bottle of water on the night-stand. My stiff fingers wrap around the thin plastic, the crackling sound piercing the heavy silence. "What are you doing here?"

"We seem to have a problem, you and I."

The room temperature water slides down my parched throat as I gulp the remnants in the bottle.

"The fact that someone tried to kill me tonight?"

His grip around the ankle tenses, signaling his annoyance. A creepy, sinister smile spreads across his lips. I press up to my elbows, putting my back against the headboard.

"That is unfortunate, but I did warn you this would be dangerous."

"I thought people would make fun of me for using the wrong fork or some shit like that, not try to kill me!"

"Well, now you know. Now, the issue I left my date tied to the bed for."

The soft skin of my palm smacks against my lips in a desperate attempt to keep my stomach contents down.

"TMI, Kyle," my fingers muffling the words.

"Just wait. You'll love it."

"You're sick," I spit back.

"And you're mine, bought and paid for, so it's a moot point. The issue is with your mother."

All annoyance and fear of the predator in the room vanish, leaving a weight of lead in my belly. "My mom? What's wrong with my mom?"

"I got an interesting call tonight from the chief of police in your shit-ass hometown."

The hand still at my mouth mutes my groan.

"Why did they call you? She's *my* mom, dammit. If something's wrong—"

"I pay a lot of hush money to that town to keep shit hidden we don't want public. You'd think you'd be more grateful." Right. Hell, he's so delusional. And this loon is about to be the president. Yay.... Sorry, America. "He didn't charge her. She's waiting in holding for you to come sort her shit out."

"What was it for?" I whisper in disbelief. Which is stupid of me. Of course she's fallen off the wagon even after I paid for those two weeks in rehab.

"Tested positive for meth plus possession, driving while intoxicated, and indecent exposure."

"Nice of her to wrap all that up in one arrest," I say on a fake laugh. "Meth? Never a dull day with that mom of mine."

"Go handle it. Tomorrow. Take the jet, but for fuck's sake, keep it out of the fucking press."

"Okay, go home, sort out Mom, come back. We need to solidify a plan for the next couple months." Mapping out the cities we want to hit in between the debates and other required appearances during the campaign is crucial to gain the votes we'll need to win.

Kyle's returning smirk sparks a warning as bright as a firework finale. "You do that, Walmart. Just handle your shit."

Wisely, I don't move an inch or even breathe too loud as he stands from the bed. After adjusting his jacket and buttoning the top button, he steps for the door. Not wanting to draw attention, I keep my unfocused gaze on the spot he vacated, ignoring his demanding stare. My skin crawls with the awareness of being watched.

"Maybe when you get back, you need a reminder of who's in power here. Because I can guaran—fucking—tee it isn't you, Walmart. Remember that, and maybe you'll survive the next four years."

TEXAS RANGERS BALL cap pulled low and chin tucked tight to my chest, I focus on my ratty Converses slapping on top of the black tarmac. Two sets of men's shoes match my steps on either side as we approach the jet. Thankfully the stairs are already down when we approach, allowing me to take the steps two at a time the moment we near the plane. Inside, I inhale deeply, scanning the partially filled cabin.

Laptop bag snug against my side, I shuffle down the aisle toward a grouping of empty seats. The seat belt clicks shut, and I tug the loose end to tighten it around my lap. Disregarding the final agents filing onboard, I adjust in the seat to stare out the window.

Outside a light fall wind blows through the trees' brightly covered leaves, loosening some with each pass and scattering them to the ground. I tug the edges of my lightweight jacket tighter. It's not cold outside by most northerner's standards, but for this Texas girl, if it's below eighty, a jacket and scarf are needed to survive.

Not that I'll need either where we're headed.

Movement draws my attention from the beautiful fall display. I take in the perfectly tailored pants lingering on the outline of thick thighs before scanning up a narrow waist, broad shoulders, tan neck —wait a second. Why in the hell am I focusing on his neck? Yes, it's kissable. Purely edible, actually.

No.

Stop it, Randi.

You will not lust after this asshole.

But I can't seem to stop myself no matter what asshole thing he does or says. Which is odd, and considering everyone else's odd is my normal, this is the oddest of oddities. Normally once I get a glimpse past the sexy exterior into the arrogant asshole that the man is at the core, I'm uninterested. Not simply turned off but revolted. But not with this agent. Oh no, that would be *way* too convenient.

The fact that I can't stop gravitating to him any time he's close should make me question his true self. Is he truly an asshat at heart or just bitter but has a good heart and soul beneath it all? Right now, with everything else going on around me, I can't dive into that theory. Later. Someday I'll work it out.

Plus, I'm his boss, right? Pretty sure an interoffice relationship is listed somewhere in the top things to avoid. Even though the mental image of us alone in a dark office, me sprawled on top of a disheveled desk with him between—

"Ma'am?"

Trouble's honey brown eyes brighten with humor, crinkling at the edges with a sunburst of lines. Whoops, I'm blatantly staring as I fantasize about an inappropriate work hookup. And I mean hookup, not relationship. Those things are way too touchy-feely for this emotionally unavailable, overworked, 'too stressed to even remember to eat' girl.

"Sorry, still a little fuzzy, I guess." Clearing my throat, I distract myself by bending forward to rifle through my laptop bag in search of my iPad. "But that's not unusual for me." Fuck, I sound like an idiot.

I swear I'm smart and can rock the VP role if I'm elected. It might be wise to have that printed on a small business card to hand out after I've said something that displays my crazy.

A curse almost slips past my lips when the sexy Secret Service guy settles into the light leather seat across the tiny table that separates us. Not sure why he chose to sit close by, considering this morning he and the rest of the guys, minus Terminator, are acting frigid toward me. Why the mood from last night—tense but casual—shifted to all business, I have no idea. Maybe I said something strange in my sleep or to an agent when he woke me up per the doctor's instructions.

I part my lips and suck in a breath, ready to ask why the cold shoulder, but seal them shut when the captain's voice comes over the speakers, informing us we're cleared for takeoff.

The row shakes, jostling me in my chair, as the massive boulder of a man settles into the seat beside me. Instinct kicks in, pulling me away from Terminator until my right shoulder hits the thick plastic window. A flash of uncertainty crosses his face. Not wanting to hurt the big guy's feelings, I stretch my lips into a tight smile. It's not him I don't want touching me, it's most people. Casual or intimate, it doesn't matter; all of it sets off an internal timer, counting down how long I must endure the contact until I can pull way.

"How's the head?" he asks. His assessing gaze sweeps along my face like he can see through to my injured brain. Sweet man.

"Still hurts, but it's not pounding toward the edge of pulverizing my brain, so that's an improvement."

A corner of his lips tugs up. "That's good. We caught the driver of the truck that caused the accident last night."

That has my full attention. Brows raised, I lean back against the plane and rest my head on the window. "Oh yeah? Has he said anything?"

"Nothing, unfortunately. We've run his name though the various databases, but we can't connect him to any watch list groups."

The building hope deflates in my chest. Blowing out through tight lips, I roll my shoulders and shift my focus from Terminator to the table. Dammit, I can't stop the disappointment from dampening my mood.

"Hey, we'll figure it out." I nod, not glancing up. "I looked over the driver's background. No way was he working alone. Until then, you're safe with us."

A large hand rests on my forearm. As I return my attention back to him, I start my internal countdown till I can move out of his grasp without it offending him. Thankfully he pulls away before the ten-second timer buzzes.

"We're your primary or alpha team. Last night was a shi—" Terminator clears his throat. "Apologies, ma'am—"

I hold up a hand to halt his apology. "Stop. I want to be myself when you and the other agents are around, and I want the same from you. All of you. I'm not some sensitive, stuck-up Washington socialite. You don't have to pussyfoot around me unless we're in public."

The entire plane tenses, the air turning stiff and heavy.

"What?" I ask, letting a hint of annoyance seep into my tone. Terminator doesn't speak up, looking everywhere other than me. I scan the cabin, looking for someone who will explain. "Okay, what is going on?"

"We believe considering your relationship with Birmingham, it's best to keep everything professional, keep the lines clear." There's no mistaking the disdain in Trouble's voice.

What the hell?

I meet his flaring gaze. "My relationship."

"Oh, I'm sorry. Are you just his fuck toy?"

"Benson!" Terminator shouts.

"You know nothing about me," I grit out. Pressing my elbow to the tabletop, I lean forward, shortening the distance between me and the judgy prick.

"I know enough."

Instead of launching across the table and wrapping my hands around his neck like I desperately want, I lean back into the seat and cross both arms across my chest. "Oh really? Go on, then, tell me a bit about myself."

His honey brown eyes darken with challenge. "You're nothing more than a pretty political pawn—"

"Aw, you think I'm pretty," I say, batting my eyelashes and pressing a hand to my heart before shooting him the bird. "And side note, I prefer Politician Barbie."

"You'll do anything that fuckstick Birmingham tells you—"

"Enough!" Terminator shouts and pushes up from his seat like he might take a swing at Trouble.

I hold out a hand to stop him. "No, let him get it out. Everyone can see he has a chip on his shoulder the size of Texas and has something to say." I swipe a hand across the table. "Well, here's your chance, Trouble. Get it out of your system now. But I will say we agree on one thing: him being a fuckstick, not me being his puppet."

"Scheming puppet—"

"Judgmental asshole."

"Fuck, can I finish?" he grits out. Not sure how, considering his teeth and jaw are locked down tight.

"Oh, please continue. This is so interesting. I love learning new awful things about myself."

"You're nothing but a fraud."

Heavy tension settles inside the plane.

Swallowing back the lump lodged in my throat, I swing my gaze to the table, breaking from his hate-filled glare. If looks could kill, I'd be bleeding out all over this fancy plane. "There is a bit of truth in that statement," I whisper, "but not in the way you're thinking."

"Enough," Terminator says in a tight, quiet voice that's more terrifying than his yell. "Benson, you will keep your opinions to yourself and keep your fat-ass mouth shut. Ma'am, I apologize for—"

"I asked for it," I say quickly to stop him. No idea why I egged him on, but I won't play innocent in the argument. It's crazy, but somehow I know he doesn't believe those terrible things about me, not deep down. I know firsthand how people treat me who truly believe what they see is what they get, and Trouble isn't one of them. He's angry, yes, and from the outburst just now, I can tell it's because he was hurt by someone who is or was a political pawn. Maybe even more than one person. Something happened to cause the man sitting across from me to become this bitter shell of the fun, mischievous person I can tell he used to be. "We're good."

Trouble's eyes widen at my words. The minuscule dip of his chin signals to our spectators that the show is over. Once again the chatter increases, vibrating around the cabin, punctuated by the insistent clicking on laptops or their phones.

"What I was trying to do before you two got into your spat was introduce you to the team."

Oops, forgot I don't know anyone's real name. "Sorry, T." I give his rock-solid shoulder an awkward pat. "Go ahead with the introductions. Trouble and I won't cause any more... well, trouble."

Pointing across the table at Trouble, he says, "Benson." Then he shifts his finger to point to the next guy. "Jenkins, Hanks, Jones, Alejo, Walsh, Cole, and Banks. I'm Washington, the team lead."

I give a small wave and awkward smile. "Randi Sawyer. Are those last names or first names?"

"Last. Now, we're your primary team going forward. If you need anything, let me know. Beta team will meet us in Dallas before driving ahead to secure the area."

I snort. "Secure the area. You're hilarious, T-man. You know where we're going, right?"

"Boone, Texas."

"Well, there are around fifteen hundred people in the town, and I can guarantee you no one there will try to hurt me. And if some random snuck in to plot another hit on me, they'd be run out of town before they could settle into the only motel. I don't want a lot of attention drawn to us." Shifting in the seat, I fiddle with the iPad resting on my lap. "You know why we're going, right?"

Terminator shoots a quick look at Trouble.

You've got to be kidding me. "Seriously? No one told you what's going on?" My gaze bounces between the two men. So different physically and, from what I've seen so far, personality wise, but the two seem to gel. Trouble is the ying to T's yang.

"Birmingham told us he ordered you home and the jet would be ready, that was it. He said you'd fill us in."

"Motherfucker," I grumble and grip the iPad to keep from flinging it across the plane. "No wonder y'all think so little of me." Peering up through my lashes, I give Trouble a sad, tight-lipped smile. "He didn't order me to go home, but he did inform me of a situation that I need to handle." I huff a fake laugh. "You said I'm a fraud. Well, you're about to learn firsthand how right you are."

CHAPTER TEN

TREY

My eyes slide across the back seat of the Suburban to Randi for the third time in the last thirty seconds. For forty minutes, we've been locked side by side with Tank—or Terminator, as she's deemed him—at the wheel. I focus back out the window to the acres and acres of open farm land. Terminator does fit him, and Trouble fits me with a capital *T*.

Not that I'll admit that to her.

The resentment and disappointment from last night fused in the early morning hours, turning to disdain. On the plane, I couldn't hold my anger back any longer, and it poured from me like water from an opened dam. Then she went and confused the hell out of me during the back-and-forth tirade. In that minute, everything I *thought* I knew about her changed. My disdain, the hate, and anger, it all receded, leaving confusion in its place.

Which is why I can't keep my eyes off her now. She's a puzzle, this Randi Sawyer, one I'm determined to solve.

Again my gaze finds its way to her side of the SUV. With her brows furrowed, her hazel eyes skim over the iPad screen, teeth chewing on her pinkie nail.

I shouldn't instigate another fight, but the last one was so entertaining. Plus I have to figure her out, and when she's pissed, her guard is down, providing a peek into the real Randi Sawyer.

"Facebook or Instagram?" I say, my tone bored.

She doesn't even glance from the screen. "How little you think of me is quite astounding. Really it is."

"Ah, you're on Twitter, catching up on the news."

I smile at the flare of her nostrils.

"No, you idiot." Sitting back in the seat, she adjusts her knees to angle to my side. Perfect. "Listen. I'm not sure what type of women you've surrounded yourself with, but based on your preconceived judgments of me, I'm guessing no one I'd be friends with. Stop trying to figure me out if you're unwilling to shove all your judgmental, idiotic, chauvinistic notions up your ass before you do. I deserve a clean fucking slate, cowboy, because I can guarantee you I'm unlike anyone you've ever met."

I smirk. "Cocky."

The tip of her ponytail swishes along her back as she shakes her head. Her pursed lips and loud sigh give off a disappointed feel.

My smile fades as lead sinks in my gut. "Then what?" I ask, desperate for the answer.

Randi sighs and nibbles on the corner of a thumbnail. "You'll figure it out soon enough." Adjusting her weight, she leans forward to point at something outside my window. "We're here." Craning my neck, I barely catch a worn sign announcing the town we're entering. "Let's see what you think of me by the end of the day."

My brows furrow at the uncertainty in her voice.

But that doesn't make sense.

Curiosity building, I shift in my seat, unable to sit still.

Tank's voice booms from the front. "Okay, ma'am—"

"I told you on the plane, T, only in public, okay? When it's just us, it's Randi. Or Rand. None of this 'ma'am' shit."

In the review mirror, his reflection smiles. An actual smile. It's unheard of for him to drop the professional mask when he's working. Tank says smiling comes off as unprofessional. It's a challenge I face daily, considering I find humor in just about everything. Well, I used to. The past few years have put me in the less humorous, more jaded category in life.

"Randi, where are we headed? You said you'd tell us when we made it to town." All traces of the earlier smile are gone, leaving his normal tense mask.

She pitches forward, our shoulders almost touching, her head between the front seats.

"What do you know about my past?"

Gremlin responds from the front passenger seat. "Grew up in Boone, Texas, pregnant at fifteen, daughter at sixteen, graduated top of your class—"

"The basics. Okay, well, if you can't tell by the current scenery, Boone isn't the wealthiest city or the biggest."

"So?" I say before I can stop myself. I need to get a fucking grip. I'm hanging on every word, desperate to learn more.

"What you've seen, who you think I am"—her hazel eyes slide to meet mine—"it's one layer, the tip of the iceberg. You're about to get a front row seat to who I've had to fight to *not* become."

For several minutes, the whirl of the tires along the asphalt fills the otherwise silent Suburban.

"I don't understand," I say, breaking the quiet.

"You will," she whispers, leaning back into the seat, her shoulders rounded and head lowered. "To answer your question, T, in two more lights, make a left and then take a right at the stop sign."

My focus shifts from her as Tank makes the various turns. Something antsy and desperate builds, begging me to grab her shoulder and pull her close.

What the actual fuck?

Comfort is not a top ten attribute of mine. Or twenty. Yet seeing her ashamed urges me to heal whatever pain is causing this strong woman to falter.

"Ma'am—" Tank clears his throat. "Randi, you sure you know where you're going?"

Her head bobs in a slight nod.

What the hell is going on?

Tearing my gaze from her side of the Suburban, I glance out the windshield and do a double take.

"The police station?"

Even with Tank's dark sunglasses, I can tell he's watching through the rearview mirror. I shrug and shake my head. No wonder she wasn't concerned with security. At least twenty cop cars and a few highway patrol SUVs fill the parking lot.

Tank eases the Suburban to the curb right outside the front door.

"I don't want to make a scene," Randi says to the window, staring at the glass doors of the station. "I'd prefer to go in alone." Tank starts to object, but she cuts him off. "But I know you won't let that happen. How about you guys stay out here, and I'll take Trouble in with me. It's safe in there, you know it is, and if anything shady happens outside, you can let Trouble know."

"I don't—"

"Please," she says on a heavy sigh. "I've done this before, unfortunately. We'll be in and out. Kyle said they didn't book her, so there shouldn't be any paperwork."

Her?

My already burning curiosity spikes. My eyes flick from Randi to the police station and back again.

"I've got her," I say, popping the door handle and shoving the heavy door open. "In and out, like she says. We're at a police station, for fuck's sake, Tank."

After slamming the door shut, I step to the driver side door and motion for him to lower the window.

"It's fine," I say reassuringly with two thumbs up and a smile.

"It's not, you fool," he growls. "You're putting her life in danger."

Gremlin shouts a curse. Both our heads whip to the other side of the SUV as two doors slam shut.

"Shit," I grumble and bolt around the hood. "Ma'am," I shout in warning just as Gremlin wraps his arms around her waist, halting her determined stride toward the doors.

"Let me go," she grunts, wiggling in his arms, unable to break free.

Gremlin's eyes lift up to mine, an unspoken question passing between us.

"Don't run off like that," I chastise, lifting the standard-issue dark sunglasses as I massage the bridge of my nose between two fingers. "It makes us look bad, and you could die. Neither is good."

Randi's fight against Gremlin's hold lessens.

I wave a hand for him to drop his restraint and hike a thumb over my shoulder. "I've got it from here. Take watch with Tank. Let me know if anything happens out here while we're inside."

With an annoyed glare directed at Gremlin's retreating back, Randi adjusts her jacket with frustrated tugs and pulls. I reach out and grip the metal door handle, pulling it open. A burst of dry heat singes up my nose and immediately dries out my throat. Fuck, it's hot in there. Just the thought of stepping into that makes me regret volunteering. September in Texas is fucking hot already; why do they have the damn heat on?

"After you," I say and sweep a hand between us. Sweat drips down my back from being sandwiched in the heat. She rolls her shoulders and shakes her hands like she's flicking out the tension, then walks through the door.

The linoleum floor squeaks with every step we take inside. I scan the waiting area; an older woman glances up from behind an aged, ragged desk. I match Randi's steps, staying inches from her back.

"Christy," Randi says, a full smile brightening her face.

The older woman, Christy apparently, smiles back. The white of her hair has a blue tint that matches the thick layer of eye shadow plastered across her eyelids. Deep wrinkles mark every inch of her face, giving her a kind, gentle look.

"Well, look who we have here. Randi Sawyer, look at you!" With a clap, the older woman slides off her stool and shuffles around the desk, both arms extended wide. Randi hesitates, muscles stiff before stepping into the woman's grasp, accepting the predestined hug.

What was that about? I step closer, curiously monitoring their interaction.

"Yeah, a bit of a change, right?" Randi gives Christy's shoulder an awkward pat and steps back, putting her at arm's length. "Somedays I don't even recognize myself." She shifts from one foot to the other, nibbling on the nail of her middle finger. "I'm somewhat pretty now."

"Randi," Christy admonishes. "You stop that right now. You've always been beautiful in the most important spot. Right here." She presses her right hand over her heart. "Now everyone can see what I've always known, sweet girl."

If I wasn't blatantly staring, I would've missed Randi's eyes flick to me before quickly going back to Christy.

"You know why I'm here?" Randi asks around the pinkie fingernail she's now nibbling on.

Christy's kind expression drops, the happy wrinkles falling and making her age instantly. "I do. Who's he?"

"Secret Service."

"Boyfriend too?"

"Christy!" Randi groans and shakes her head. "Stop it. That would be inappropriate."

"Why?" Christy blurts. I chuckle into the fist at my lips. "He has a sweet face."

"Thank you." I step forward, hand extended. "Trey Benson, Secret Service, ma'am. Pleased to meet you."

I barely grasp her frail hand, afraid even a gentle squeeze will break bones.

"My, my, aren't you a charmer. Trouble, that's what you are," she says with a wink.

"That's what I said," Randi grumbles beside me.

"Don't let this one push you around, you hear?" Christy says, nodding toward the huffing Randi. "She's got a good soul, a good heart. Best thing to come out of this town, if you ask me. She don't deserve the life she was handed."

I half turn to meet Randi's eyes, my brows raised in question, but they're too busy inspecting the blank, white wall to notice.

A puzzle indeed. All the pieces aren't adding up. Only way to solve this is to ask the right questions.

"Is that so?" I tuck both hands behind my back, my lips pulling up in a wide smile to Christy. Hopefully a little charm will open her up. "Seems like a pretty great life to me. UT, Harvard, on her way to being vice president."

Christy's eyes narrow. Shaking her head, she looks to Randi. "Cute but not that bright."

"Agreed."

"Hey now." What the hell? This is not going as planned. I glance between the two women. "Don't gang up on me. Just an observation."

"I'm worried for her safety if those are your observation skills, son."

Well hell. Did I just get smack-talked by an eighty-year-old lady?

"Leave him alone," Randi says, still smiling, clearly laughing at me. "You know why he doesn't know. It's why Mom's in holding instead of booked already."

The woman grunts in agreement.

"Wait," I state and turn to face Randi. "Your mom is *here*. In holding?"

She nods with a noncommittal shrug. "Not the first time either."

"Come on. I'll take you to her." The keys jingle as Christy's trembling hand slides the key into the lock and tugs the door open. Halfway down the narrow hall, she calls over her shoulder, "Everything else has been taken care of by that evil man of yours."

"She mean's Kyle," Randi says back to me.

"Take it you don't like him," I shout as we turn a corner, taking another short hall.

She shakes her head, her silver-blue hair bouncing with the movement. "Anyone can see through his charm. A wolf in sheep's clothing, if you ask me. If it weren't for Randi here, no way I'd want him in office."

"You and most Americans," Randi mutters, not bothering to turn to make sure I hear her.

"Here we are." Christy's hand pauses over the doorknob. With a resigned sigh, she turns to Randi, sympathy etched across her face. "I know you've tried to help her, but, Randi, some people just aren't ready for what we're so willing to give. You hear me? Your mother has made her own life choices, and you've made yours. She does not define you. Never has and never will. Now get your mama home and get your ass back to DC. Do something about those ridiculous damn taxes. I work hard for my money, don't want that government taking any more than they already are."

"Yes, ma'am." Rolling her shoulders, Randi stretches her neck to the right, then left. "Okay, I'm ready. Let's do this."

Why does it feel like we're about to go into battle?

"Do we need backup?" I question, though it feels stupid to suggest I can't handle her mom on my own.

Hazel eyes meet mine, flicking from one to the other, searching for… hell if I know.

"Maybe."

What the hell?

CHAPTER ELEVEN

RANDI

Dammit, why did I ask him to walk me in here? Anyone but him. Internally I groan and turn back to the door Christy's unlocking. I'm not embarrassed about him seeing Mom; no that's something I got over a long time ago. It's everything Christy pointed out. Love that woman, but today I wish she'd keep her thoughts to herself. Trouble doesn't seem like the type of guy who needs his ego inflated any more than it already is.

The last thing I need right now is for him to think I find him attractive. The thin veil of anger keeping us apart needs to stay. Period. If he changes his attitude toward being kind and non-assy, I'll have a difficult time keeping my walls up. And those suckers are needed to survive the piranha-infested pond known as the DC political circle.

Relaxing both hands at my sides, I give them a quick shake, releasing the tension.

Christy pushes the door wide and steps aside, allowing me to walk in first. With a deep breath for courage, I step through. That same breath whooshes out at the sight of Mom passed out on the far side of the holding cell. All thoughts of Trouble at my back, wondering what he's thinking, vanish as I step closer and wrap my hands around the bars. The cold metal bites into my palms as I squeeze so tight my knuckles turn white.

Every time I see Mom, there is less and less of the woman I used to know left behind. The woman curled on her side on top of the lone metal bench is nothing but a shell of the charismatic woman she once was. Much thinner than the last time I saw her. Bones protrude, almost slicing through the thin skin covering her hips and shoulders. Deep lines mark her face, making her look ten years older.

The clanging of metal against metal draws my focus from Mom to Christy opening the holding cell door.

"Thank you," I whisper as I slip past. The overwhelming smell of urine, stale smoke, and decay halts my steps halfway into the cell. I raise an arm and bury my nose into the crook of my elbow before stepping closer.

"Mom," I say, muffled by the sleeve of my jacket. My chest expands as I take in a deep breath before pulling my arm away. "Mom."

Nothing.

Eyes focused on her chest, I squat low, watching for signs of life. A flash of relief settles and I release the held breath at the rapid rise and fall of her chest. At least she's alive. Forgetting about the stench wafting off Mom, I take a breath to call her name again. Nausea brews and I gag, instinctively shoving backward to move away from the stench. My ass hits the unforgiving cement floor.

Strong hands tuck under each armpit and haul me upright. The movement disrupts my already delicate equilibrium, and I sway once my feet meet the floor.

"What happened? Are you okay? Randi?"

I blink a couple times, attempting to make the room stop spinning. "Fine. I'm fine. I'm just… still a little dizzy from last night." Again, the room whirls in my vision, but this time it's due to Trouble flipping me around so we're chest to chest, his intense, assessing gaze scanning my face. "It's the smell. Really, I'm okay."

Still he doesn't release his hold. Heat floods from his warm body into my own. His hands slide from my shoulders to grip my waist, and my breath catches. Our eyes locked on one another's, everything else in the room fades. For a moment, I forget where we are and the fact that I'm comfortable in someone's hold. His honey eyes flash, opening up like a window into his soul. He's sucking me in, making me want to dive into his past to learn how he became the bitter man he is today.

"This isn't the first time, is it?" he whispers.

I shake my head. My gaze falls to his full lower lip, and I bite my own to keep from leaning forward and taking a nip.

With his chest pressed against mine, I feel the jolt of his breath catching.

"Why didn't you say something?"

I furrow my brows. "Would it have changed anything?"

"Well, yeah. I didn't know... I thought...."

"You thought you had me all figured out." Reality snaps back to the forefront of my mind. Jerking out of his hold, I turn my back to him. The intensity of his stare burns the back of my neck. I rub at it, trying to ease the feel of being watched. "Now you'll move me from one stigma to another. Nothing changes. Nothing ever changes when it comes to people's beliefs on who I am."

"I'm sorry," he says. The sympathy dripping from those two words begs me to turn back around, to step back into that warm hold.

"I don't need your pity," I bite back. I lock gazes with Christy, who's still outside the cell watching. "Do you have any extra clothes?" I nod toward my passed-out mother. "I can't take her out in that. It smells too bad. I'll puke in the car before we even leave the parking lot."

My shoulders drop at the saddened shake of her head.

"Honey, my clothes will be a tent on your mama."

She's right, but it was worth a try. Sighing, I return my focus to Mom to keep from turning back to Trouble. Why, oh why, does the one person whose touch I'm not annoyed by have to be his? And why am I desperate to snuggle against his chest and stay there for eternity? Maybe I magically got high from the drug stench seeping off Mom.

That's totally a thing.

"Benson, can you run out and grab my bag? I'll use the spare set of clothes I brought in case we need to stay overnight."

"I'm not leaving you. Tank would shit a brick." I snort in response. His clipped directives echo off the bare cinder block walls as he talks to the agents outside. "Three minutes," he says to me once he's finished. "Christy, would you meet them at the door so they can get back here?"

I'm still staring at Mom when the door snickers shut, signaling Christy's departure. Neither Trouble nor I say a word as we wait. Breathing through my mouth, I approach the bench once again and squat, putting my face close to Mom's. Minutes pass of me stroking her stringy hair before a gentle hand rests on my shoulder. Turning on the balls of my feet, I find one of the agents from the plane now standing on the other side of the bars, eyes on Mom, holding a bag in one hand.

"I'll help," Trouble says beside me.

Cutting my eyes up, I shake my head. "No thanks. I can do it."

His grip on my shoulder tightens a fraction. "It wasn't a question. Walsh," he shouts. "Drop the bag and get out. I'll help Miss Sawyer and let you know when we're ready to move out."

The bag thumps to the floor, and Christy and Walsh exit the room. Alone again, Trouble snags the bag from across the room and hauls it deeper into the holding cell, dropping it at my feet. I unzip the top zipper and search through the duffel's contents. Selecting an older pair of Wranglers and a long-sleeve T-shirt, I pile them on top of the bag and push off the cold concrete to stand.

"I'll hold her and you undress, then redress her?" I suggest. I turned down his offer to help seconds ago, but I'm thankful he didn't give me the option. Doing this alone would take forever. A challenge I'm not up to taking on right now.

I shift angles a couple times, trying to figure out the best approach to help her sit up. With Trouble's assistance, we raise her to a some-what sitting position, leaning against the wall, while I hold her shoulders so she doesn't slump forward.

"Do you want to talk about it?" he asks as he slowly peels Mom's tank top up her belly.

I cringe at the number of visible ribs beneath her pale thin skin as he pulls the ratty tank over her head. I give a half shrug in answer to his previous question. My head tilts up at Trouble's pointed cough. His cheeks are flushed pink, eyes a little wild. I follow his embarrassed gaze down to Mom's naked chest.

"Classy, Mom. Even if you don't have boobs, you still have to wear something." I shake my head and motion for him to hand me the sweater. "I can do it."

"It's fine, just didn't expect it. Hell, didn't expect any of the last thirty minutes, or twenty-four hours, honestly."

I scoff. "You've never had to bail a parent out or redress them after a drug-induced stupor?"

"That would be a definite 'never.'"

"That's a luxury I've never been afforded. It hasn't always been this bad, but it's never been good, that's for sure."

"Lay her back against the bench and make sure she doesn't roll off while I get her shorts off." His fingers pause at the button. "Uh, Randi?"

I glance up. I almost laugh at the uncomfortable cringe he's sporting. "What?"

"Just wanting to prepare myself here. Think the underwear situation is the same down here as it was up top?"

Now I can't help but laugh, then immediately gag. Shit, this place stinks. No. Mom reeks.

"It's fifty-fifty, honestly. You never know with this one." I stifle another giggle at his full-body shudder. "Come on. Let's get this over with and get her home."

THANK goodness it's not as cold here as it was in DC. This pleasant fall day at eighty–five degrees allows us to ride with the windows rolled down in the Suburban as we drive to Mom's. The change of clothes helped but not by much; the overpowering stench of stale smoke and body odor still wafts off her in waves.

The leather seat creaks as I lean forward to tap T on the shoulder. "It's your next right." Through the windshield, I watch the sign for Green Meadows come into view. The G is missing, and Meadows now says dows, but hey, it's home.

Was home.

T slows to make the turn but slides to a complete stop instead of turning into the run-down trailer park.

"Randi?"

"Yes, T. Here."

"Here?"

"Here."

"Randi, this is a—"

"Run-down trailer park. I know this. Believe me, I know exactly what it is. I'm the one who grew up here, after all."

"Here?"

"I thought we already covered that."

Trouble chuckles in the seat beside me, making me smile. At least someone gets my humor. Grumbling under his breath, T eases his foot off the brake and turns the SUV into the entrance.

"Okay, it's the third one on the left." I crane my neck to see out the window as we pass a turnoff, hoping for a glimpse of my old trailer.

"What's down there?" Trouble asks, leaning forward to look through my window too. "Old boyfriend's house?"

"Um, no."

"Then what? You were looking for something."

I lift my hand toward my mouth and nibble on the thumbnail. "Mine."

"Your what?"

"My trailer," I whisper, then cut my eyes at him to gauge his reaction.

A deep line creases between his neat brown brows as his eyes flick from me to the window and back again.

Before I can ask what he's thinking, we pull to a stop. A pained groan fills the back of the car. Everyone tenses but doesn't make a move. We're all probably thinking the same thing—maybe she'll pass back out.

No such luck.

Which shouldn't be a surprise. We are talking about my luck, after all. I thought my shitty luck changed when we won the damn primary, only to be painfully reminded the win locked me into an indebted contract with a dirty politician. Go me. Maybe if I wouldn't have been so focused on proving myself to my haters I would've realized the bear trap I was walking right into.

Another groan with unintelligible mumbled words fills the third row. I pull my knees into my seat and press a cool cheek against the headrest. Glassy, bloodshot eyes blink up but don't focus.

How long will it take for her come down from a meth high? She's always been an addict at worst, alcoholic at best, but she was a good mom. As good as she could be, I guess. Not great, but it could've been worse.

"Mom. You're okay. It's me, Randi. You're home."

A wet cackle rattles her chest, and I cringe back an inch. "Randi. I missed you, honey."

Right, and a Texas summer isn't hot.

"Let's get her inside." I turn to open the door but pause at Trouble's eyes focused on me. "What?"

He shakes his head and throws the door open like it pissed him off somehow. Before I can do the same, mine opens on its own with T just outside the door. I nod in thanks and slide out to access the back seat where Mom's laid out. Without a word, T reaches into the back and carefully slides Mom out, cradling her tiny frame in his arms.

Warm tears fill my lower lids as I stare at the two. His larger-than-life size dwarfing hers making her body look so tiny and frail.

My lips purse to keep the building emotions shoved down deep where they belong. Tonight I can break down. When I'm alone later, I can freak out and cry over the last twenty-four hours. Until then, I keep my shit together. No showing weakness.

"Okay, then," I croak, the rising emotions stealing my voice. *Dammit! Keep your shit together, Randi.*

Dead grass crunches beneath my Converses as I turn to my old home and march for the front door. My stomach lurches into my throat when the first step cracks beneath my weight. Moving slower, I gingerly step onto the next wooden stair, testing it before putting my full weight on the rotting wood. "Good to know the money I've sent you has gone to good use," I grumble.

I knew better then to send her money, but she's my mom, and I had it, so I sent her some when she was in a bad spot. I clearly remember those 'bad spot' days, or years for me; I couldn't turn her away empty-handed.

Stepping on the landing, I crack my neck and grasp the flimsy metal door handle. I pause, staring at the clouded window. What will the inside look like if the outside is the start of a horror film? The handle wiggles in my grasp. There's a screech of rusted metal bending, and then the door flies open. Adrenaline explodes from my belly, shooting scorching heat through my veins. I curse, jolting back to keep the door from giving me tetanus. Losing my footing, I stumble back a step. Arms flailing, I take another step back, only to meet air instead of more rotten wood.

Swinging my arms in large circles, I attempt to fight gravity from taking me down.

But like always, that bitch wins.

CHAPTER TWELVE

RANDI

The air whistles from my lungs, my neck snapping back against something solid.

"Fuck." A hot breath brushes through my hair, floating it across my face.

Heart in my throat, I take a breath and hold it to calm down before I stroke out. My entire body trembles, but I stay upright due to strong arms banded around my waist. A pleasant spicy scent hits my nose. *Hmm, that smells nice.* I take another deep whiff, my eyes rolling back in my head at the desire that sparks from the scent alone. To my credit, my odd behavior could be from aggravating last night's head trauma by cracking it again on... wait, what did I crack it on?

Following the mix of citrus and cinnamon, I sniff the air a few times, following it until my nose smacks into a solid, suit-covered chest.

"Seriously?" A deep chuckle vibrates Trouble's chest, tickling my own. "Did you just sniff me? Maybe we should get your head checked again."

"Probably wouldn't be a terrible idea," I mutter with my nose still buried in the soft fabric of his jacket. "Just one more sniff."

"Baby!"

The magical bubble his scent surrounded me in bursts. His arm tightens a fraction before helping me step out of his hold to stand on my own. I turn, a snarl pulling at my lips at the man standing on the landing.

"What in the hell are you doing here?" I demand. My fingers curl into tight fists at my side. "Mom, what is he doing here? Did you call him baby?" My gaze doesn't leave the piece-of-shit slimeball standing just outside Mom's trailer door. A sleazy smile spreads across his pockmarked cheeks, displaying what remains of his teeth—which isn't much.

"Well, I'll be fucking damned." A shiver runs down my spine as realization dawns. "Shoulda known she'd get your skinny ass out of jail."

"Ma'am?"

I reluctantly pull my attention from Jimmy, our small town's main drug dealer, to T. Mom wiggles in his arms, attempting to get away, eyes only for Jimmy.

"This can't be happening," I mutter. I gesture toward the ground for T to set her down. What other choice do I have? Make her come back to DC with me? Hell no. That town isn't ready for Mom's shit show life.

Her bare feet barely touch the ground before she wobbles toward the trailer, stumbling up the two steps only to fall face first on the landing. Jimmy chuckles as her frail arms give out under her light weight each time she tries to push up.

"Mom." She ignores me. "Mom!" I shout and step closer to the trailer. A tight grip on my bicep prevents me from moving closer. Whipping around, I scowl at Trouble. "I need to help her."

The shake of his head is barely noticeable. Eyes on the two addicts, he steps closer, putting his chest against my back. "Who is he?" The tension in his voice, the silent command, brings the whole situation into focus.

I glance around, looking at each of the agents. Everyone stands close, tension radiating off their stiff postures, hands at their hips in case they need their weapons quickly.

Shit, didn't think how this looks to them. To me it's a common scene. No doubt this is a first for them.

"Mom's new boyfriend, apparently. That's Jimmy Caster, criminal and drug dealer." A demanding throb pulses through my head. I tip my hat back and press both palms to my temples to ease the pain. It doesn't help.

"Damn, woman," Jimmy says, drawing my reluctant attention back to him. Bile rises up my throat at the sight of Mom hanging on his bony shoulders, rubbing herself against his side. "Look at ya." My back vibrates at Trouble's low growl. "Come on inside and I'll show ya what you been missin' out on." Mom giggles beside him. Fucking giggles. He tilts his head down to her. "If yer a good girl, maybe I won't tell everyone about your mama here."

My stomach lurches. This time there's no stopping it. Squatting to the grass, I vomit the water and bits of food from the light breakfast on the plane.

Shit, this is bad.

"Get her out of here," Trouble orders.

I don't fight it as I'm hauled up to a standing position and directed away from the trailer toward the Suburban. A blast of cold air at the open door has goose bumps pebbling my skin. A gentle hand presses against my lower back, urging me inside.

"I can't leave her like that," I tell Gremlin as realization dawns. "I can't leave her with him."

"We'll handle it, ma'am."

"This can't get out to the press. Kyle will kill me," I whisper.

"We'll handle it." A commotion draws my attention, but Gremlin stops me from looking around the door with a gentle hand to my cheek. "Sounds like Benson already is, ma'am. She'll be fine, but we need you safe, and that's inside here. Understand?"

I swallow down the lump clogging my throat. *Do not cry, Randi. Not here. Not yet.*

With a shaky nod, I climb inside the SUV and slide onto the soft leather seat. "Thank you." Meeting his light blue eyes, I attempt a grateful smile.

I expect to see pity written across his face and in his gaze, but instead all I find is something like compassion. With a quick nod, he shuts the door, enclosing me inside alone. An agent stands on either side of the passenger doors while the rest of the team forms a short line, shoulders touching, blocking my line of sight to the trailer. After a few minutes of gnawing on my thumbnail almost to the quick, the line finally breaks apart. T and Trouble wear similar grim expressions as they approach the SUV, Gremlin following, while the other agents march to the second Suburban and file in.

I keep silent, my frantic gaze flicking between the three men as they climb in. Unseeing gaze focused on my clasped hands, I clear my throat, trying to ease the tension-filled quiet. Everything feels heavy. I need one hour alone to process it all.

"I want to stay overnight in Dallas." My voice breaks from the lump of unshed tears in my throat. "We'll go home tomorrow."

"Ma'am, Mr. Birmingham said—"

Anger washes away the pity party I was starting at the mention of his name. Snapping my gaze up, I meet T's dark sunglasses in the rearview mirror. "I don't give a fuck what Kyle wants right now. I need one night away, an hour alone to deal with all this shit. Do you realize what happened last night?"

"Someone tried to off you."

I side-eye Trouble. "I was thinking about how I somehow won to potentially become the second most powerful person in the country, but yeah, toss me almost dying in there too. And this today." I shake my head and immediately regret it. I squeeze my head between my palms, attempting to alleviate the throbbing. "I can't go back tonight. Plus, I have to figure out how to fucking keep Jimmy quiet and what to do with Mom—"

"It's taken care of."

I shift in the seat, angling toward Trouble.

"What does that mean?"

"I made sure he understands the consequences if he speaks to the press." His shoulders rise and fall in a shrug, but his eyes won't meet mine.

"And that means what, exactly?"

"He beat the shit out of that fucker and told him worse would happen if he said anything about your mom." My eyes widen at Gremlin's words. "Oh, and told him to stay away from your mom."

"What the hell?" Too many conflicting emotions pour through me to decipher which one I actually feel. Happy, angry, sad, relieved.

Again, he shrugs.

"Look at me, dammit." I smack his shoulder to get his attention. "Seriously?"

Only the barest outline of his eyes is visible through his dark sunglasses, but I know he's watching me.

"He was a threat to you, so we handled the situation."

"Um, did anyone else throw a punch?"

He smirks and shakes his head.

"Then *you* handled the situation." Pinching pain fills my lower lip as I bite down. "What about Mom? She'll just go right back to him, and I'll be back down here next week hauling her out of holding. Again."

"Rehab."

I let out a sarcastic laugh. "Been there, done that. It doesn't stick."

"There are several good ones out in California. They have a higher success rate than others because of the long programs."

I purse my lips and raise both brows high on my forehead. "You seem to know a lot about it. Been recently?"

Silence.

Interesting. Interesting indeed.

"I've looked into those before, but if I remember right, they were way too expensive for what I could afford," I tell him.

"What about Birmingham?" All warmth from his features disappears at the mention of Kyle. "Won't he help you with your mom?"

I shake my head and turn to look out the window. "I don't want any more reason to be indebted to that asshole. I need to do this on my own."

It would make life a lot simpler if I asked Kyle for the money, but what would he demand in return? I'm already in too deep as it is with him and his corrupt family.

"I'll figure it out," I murmur to the glass. "I always do."

THE SUITE IS ridiculous in the best way possible. Every surface shines while light sparkles around the room. Sweet vanilla mixed with jasmine fills my nose as I step deeper into the living room. I shift on my feet, staring at the floral carpet while attempting to keep the tears I've held for hours at bay for a few more minutes as the guys secure the room.

Absurd if you ask me. It's not like this was a planned stop. Deciding to stay overnight at The Ritz in downtown Dallas before flying out tomorrow was too impromptu for someone to plan a master assassination attempt. The guys fought me in the car, saying it would be best if we went on home tonight, but using my award-winning debate skills I won the argument.

Hopefully Kyle won't ream them for going against his direct orders. He'll be furious with me, but I don't give two flying fucks. I need a hot bath, a Snickers bar, and no fewer than two boxes of tissue to get through the next hour. All these damn emotions need an outlet before I explode in a river of tears and a gooey mess of snot.

I never cry, but the previous twenty-four hours would get to anyone with a pulse.

"Clear," T's booming voice echoes through the room.

Almost like my tears know relief is coming soon, two escape, slowly rolling down my hot cheeks. Gaze lowered, I race to the master bedroom. The fancy-ass door refuses to close quickly even as I shove on it, desperate for privacy. With only an inch to go, the sense of someone watching draws my attention. On the other side of the door, Trouble's worried face fills the remaining small gap. His lips part, but the door clicks shut before he can get out a single word.

The worry and confusion shining from his light brown eyes snap the thin restraint on my rolling emotions. Tossing the ball cap to the bed, I fall to the floor not caring that I'm falling apart in the middle of the room. My ass hits the soft carpet. Knees tucked to my chest, I press my forehead to my thighs and let the tears flow.

Seconds. Minutes. Hell, maybe hours pass, but I don't move.

Something taps my shoulder startling me out of my hysteria. Peeling my forehead away from my jeans at a gentle touch on my shoulder, uncomfortable dark brown eyes watch from where T is crouched beside me. It's stupid, and so unlike me, but instead of pulling away from his comforting grip, I lean in to it. Happy-filled tingles spark from his touch. It's nothing like the heat and desire that coursed through my veins from Trouble's, but still, the sense of support fills my heart with a friendly calm.

"You okay?" he asks.

Breaking his gaze, I rest my chin on my knees. A breath catches in my chest at the sight of Trouble, also in the room, perched on the edge of the large four poster bed.

"This won't be a thing, will it?" he asks, crossing his arms over his chest. The annoyed look on his face is almost believable if it weren't for the deep crease between his brows signaling the concern that lurks beneath the facade.

"And what would that be?" I sniffle and discreetly wipe my nose across my jeans in attempts to look somewhat presentable.

He waves in my direction with a pointed look to my tear smeared face. "The crying."

"For fuck's sake, Benson." Pure exasperation fills T's tone.

A genuine laugh tickles my chest, making the tears slow. "Fuck, I hope not. But if every day for the next couple months or worse four years is like the last twenty-four hours, I can't give you any promises." My teeth sink into the nail of my pinkie. "It won't be, right?"

Both men huff. "Sure as hell hope not. It's been a day of firsts for us too."

"Does that mean I win some kind of prize?"

"For what?" Trouble asks, his signature sexy smirk on full display.

"Being the biggest mess in the shortest amount of time." I flick my gaze between the two men. "Come on. I deserve something for adding some excitement to your mundane lives, right?"

T drops his head with a hint of a smile on his lips. "And what kind of prize were you thinking?"

"Candy, of course." Duh.

"Chocolate?" His voice rises, his eyes wide.

"Down, boy." Trouble laughs. "This is for her, not you."

"You like chocolate?" I can't help my growing smile. He looks like a guy who would snack on bullets or whole turkey legs, not chocolate. "We're going to be good friends, you and I."

"Friends?" His eyes narrow. "We're here to protect you, not be your friends."

Tears well again. Fuck, why does that hurt so bad?

"Idiot," Trouble mutters. His heavy footsteps pause in front of my Converse. "And you're the married one. Sometimes I feel sorry for Sarah." T grunts something in return I don't make out. "I'll take care of Hot Mess here. You go get her something to eat. It's been a while since breakfast."

T grumbles through his groans of pain as he stands and heads out of the room. The door softly clicks behind him.

"Come on." Trouble extends a hand down, wiggling his fingers in front of my face. "Get off the floor and I'll find you something better than chocolate."

I seal my lips to suppress my smile. The same lusty heat from earlier sweeps through my body when I slide my hand into his. One swift pull and I'm standing with one hand pressed against his chest, the other still wrapped in his. My heart pounds, pulse skyrocketing at our close proximity. Tipping my head up, I zero in on his soft, plump lower lip that begs to be nibbled on.

Holy hell, I'm in deep shit.

CHAPTER THIRTEEN

TREY

Maybe I'm the one with the concussion.

What the hell is wrong with me? This woman is everything I've written off in life. Well, that's not entirely true, now that I've seen the truth. Even if she's not like all the other backstabbing, opportunistic women I've known, she's still a fucking mess.

A cute mess, if I'm honest with myself.

Even now I should be turned off by her red-rimmed eyes, black streaks of mascara down her soft cheeks, and bright red nose. But I'm not. She's adorable, not revolting.

This is bad news. T will have a heart attack if he even gets a whiff that I'm attracted to this woman who we're to protect with our lives. Which I will, without a doubt. Me thinking she's hot and wanting to feel that skin hidden beneath all those layers…

Do not think about her naked.

Do not think about her naked.

"I need a shower to get mom's stench off me."

"Not helping," I grit out.

"Huh?" She shrugs out of my hold leaving the sense of an empty void in her place. Thank fuck she did though, I wasn't going to let her go on my own. Her hazel eyes scan the entirety of the room. Hooking her thumb in the direction of the bathroom she says, "I'll just go—"

"No." There's no way I can focus on her safety with her on the other side of the door, gloriously naked and waiting for me. Maybe not that last part, but that's where my dirty imagination will take me. I give my head a shake to pull it from the gutter. "Sit." I point to the small sitting area on the other side of the room. "Wait until Tank comes back with the food. Until then, I promised you something to take the edge off."

Arms crossed across her chest, she shuffles to the low butter-cream-colored armchair and ungracefully plops into it. I hold back a laugh. This woman is proving the exact opposite of who I assumed she was. It puts me on uneven footing. All the women I've known are perfection personified. Graceful, manipulative, delicate, and vindictive —*that* I know how to defend against. But this? Her?

I pull one cabinet door open and then another before finding what I'm looking for. When I open the fridge, the cold air slides across my face feeling amazing against my heated skin. Earlier the boys turned down the air conditioning for Randi, we've all already picked up on her being cold natured, which means we're all roasting.

"White or red wine?" I call out over my shoulder loud enough for her to hear across the room.

"Tequila?"

"Damn," I mumble, a small smile pulling up the corners of my lips. Grabbing a small bottle of tequila, I slam the fridge door shut with a soft kick, then the cabinet. "You're a surprise at every turn, aren't you?"

"I'm taking that as a compliment." Our fingers graze as I hand off the tequila, shooting a bolt of want straight to my cock.

Fuuuuck.

A pop then crackle of the seal breaking sounds at my back as I move toward the bathroom. "You should. It's different for sure."

"Different how?" Her voice barely carrying over the running water wetting the cloth in my hand. After ringing it out, I step back into the bedroom and lean a shoulder against the doorframe.

"Here." I toss the wet rag across the room only for her to duck, a loud smack and squeak filling the room as it slides down the glass window behind her. "You were supposed to catch that."

"Right." Bending over the arm of the chair, she stretches to the floor, offering a great view of her round ass. I advert my gaze, pretending I wasn't staring when she pops back up, face flushed with the washcloth in hand. "What's this for?"

I maneuver a finger in the air circling in the direction of her face with a cringe. "You've got...."

A bright pink blush tints her cheeks as she dips her face to the washcloth and gives it a good scrub. "You didn't answer my question. Different how?"

Shifting my attention to the floor as she cleans up, I say, "I was wrong about who you are. I assumed you were like every other beautiful woman in DC."

"Beautiful," she says, her tone disbelieving. "And what's that?"

"You'll find out soon enough. Being different is a good thing, Randi. Don't lose it."

At her silence, I look up to find her now clean face tipped up with the small bottle pressed to her lips. A loud laugh slips past before I can stop it. Still chugging the golden liquid, her eyes cut over. The plump lips wrapped around the glass twitch upward.

"You know what? I don't think we have anything to worry about." I'm still laughing as I squat in front of the cabinet once again and retrieve another round, this time snagging a bottle of vodka for myself. Beta team took over an hour ago, so technically I'm off the clock.

"Catch it this time," I say holding up the bottle with a wink.

Her eyes narrow in concentration as she wiggles in the seat and extends both hands. "Ready."

"Wow." Never in my life have I been this entertained by a woman —with her clothes, on that is. "Here it comes. Nice and slow."

"That's not what she said." She chuckles to herself. "Not me, but any other she." Her eyes flick up to mine, and I smile while shaking my head in disbelief.

"You're kind of funny," I say, still smiling, the tequila still gripped between two fingers not wanting to make the move to hand it over. There's something special, bonding even, in this moment I don't want to interrupt.

"Really?" Hope and disbelief fill her voice. "Most people just think I'm crazy."

"Well, you're that too, but funny mostly. It's a clever funny, so I guess you have to be as smart as you to get your humor."

Her teeth sink into her lower lip. "I like that theory. I'll allow it."

"Thanks." I chuckle. "You'd rather it be hard and fast?"

"Sex or the bottle you're about to throw?"

"Sex." This is a terrible idea, but she started it. It's an excuse I can still use as an adult, right?

"Not that I remember that well," she mumbles. "But yeah, fast for sure. The quicker it's done the better."

My hand tightens around the bottle so it doesn't tumble to the floor. "I don't get that joke."

She tosses her head back with a laugh only to wince and grip her head between her hands. "Stop stalling and toss me that bottle. I need it." Her movements stiffen. "Wait, you wouldn't happen to have a cigarette on you, would you?"

"One of the guys might, but—"

"Bring the bottles." With a smile, she unfolds from the pretzel she'd scrunched into. Snatching her hat off the bad and tugging it down low, she heads to the door. "Hurry. I'm scared for my safety if this is as fast as you move."

Leaning against the living room door, I wait as I watch Randi shuffle around the room, asking each of the beta team agents for a smoke. A younger guy cautiously pulls a pack from his pocket and slides it into her hand. With her intentions clear, I tell one of the agents to go on ahead and secure the kitchen employee entrance. T shoots daggers from where he's sprawled out on the couch, no doubt needing a few minutes of sleep before room service arrives.

I slide both bottles into my pockets before raising my hands palms out. "She'll be fine. I'll go down with her."

"That doesn't make me feel better. I'm just as concerned about you two killing each other as an outside threat."

Randi snorts. "Wise man, but we're good. For now. But if he does kill me, I won't hold it against you, T."

"Yeah, because you'll be dead."

"Right, so I'll haunt him, obviously." I laugh at the sarcastic scrunch of her tiny nose. "Come on, Trouble."

Tank groans. "This is a terrible idea. I'm going with you."

"Now you're insulting me," I say, all humor gone. "Stay here, wait for the food. You know you ordered yourself something on the side. We're all starving."

"We skipped lunch," he snaps back. Yep, the man needs to eat. No one wants to be around this guy when he's hungry and tired. Terrible combo. He's my best friend and even I don't want to be near him when he's like this.

"Damn. That's my fault, isn't it?" Her eyes flick around the room, gauging the rest of the team. We all look worn the fuck out. It's obvious to her too, if the cringe she's sporting means anything. "When I'm stressed, I forget to eat. Old habits, I guess. How does this work? You guys eat when I eat or only when you're off?"

"We rotate while on shift usually, but today was a—"

"Complete mess," Randi cuts in.

"Anomaly." Tank's stress lines fade into a somewhat smile. Damn, what is it with this woman? How in the hell is she able to get to this softer side of him? "We'll figure it out, get into a routine. Now that we know you need a reminder of when to eat, that helps us. We didn't say anything today because we figured you didn't want to stop."

Randi shoves both hands to her hips. "Let's set up some rules. First, if you don't know something, ask. I don't like that you guys were starving today because you didn't ask. Second, no more of this ma'am bullshit from any of you, even in public. I swear I feel the gray hairs multiplying every time one of you says it, and I already spend way too much money on covering that shit as it is. Got it?"

Something flares in my chest at the stubborn and commanding

tone in her voice. Maybe she can do the VP thing. If she can own Tank, how much harder can running the country be?

A random thought pushes through my thoughts. What if she's this commanding in bed? My lips tug down in a frown. Hopefully not. Watching her own the room is hot as hell, but alone, I want her begging for it.

The two of them continue the rules discussion as I walk to the door, discreetly adjusting myself to hide the semi I'm sporting. These next four years will be torture if I'm like this every time I'm near her. Good thing she's with Birmingham and the job or I'd pin her against a wall the first moment we were alone. Or even if we weren't. Hell, that would be hot, the risk of being caught. Past girlfriends worried about their reputation or someone seeing too much to be... adventurous.

"Ready?"

I cut my eyes to her at the touch of humor in the single word.

Shit, how long has she been there and I failed to notice? That's not good. If I can't keep my focus, I can't keep her safe. Which is my motherfucking job. Shit.

I have to maintain distance whether my dick has other options or not. Her life depends on it.

Ignoring her pointed look I shift my attention on the hallway door and yank on the handle. The two agents outside the door stiffen, assuming full alert at her presence. Both flank us down the narrow hall and into the employee elevator, which is held, waiting, by another agent.

We stand stiff, as still as statues as the elevator descends while she shifts from one foot to the other. We're used to this. It's what we live for. Protection, constantly on high alert. The rush you get when out in public, needing your eyes on everyone and everywhere at once, provides the perfect high for an adrenaline junkie.

Like me.

Humid heat assaults me as we push the kitchen's swinging doors open, and my steps falter. Sweat builds along my forehead, a light trickle already dripping down my spine. Employees perk up from their stations as we move down the line, marching toward the back door. One glaring look and the curious glances shift away, focusing back on their work.

Good.

They should be afraid. We're all packing multiple weapons and are proficient in multiple types of hand-to-hand combat. Of course, I hope it doesn't come down to a fight, since my fists are tender from beating the shit out of that idiot earlier. I couldn't stop myself. The second his yellowed eyes raked down Randi, the leash I keep on my self-restraint snapped. Tank was beyond pissed but didn't stop it from happening, even though I broke a very fundamental rule.

One of the beta team agents files out the door first. Randi makes to follow, but with a hand to her waist, I tug her back to me.

"Wait until we get the all clear," I say into her hair. My eyes dart across the kitchen. Tension builds and my muscles tighten, readying for a fight. The agent beside me meets my gaze and nods. One hand pressed to her lower back, I push against the metal bar, releasing the latch keeping it closed.

A cool breeze swipes across my sweaty brow, instantly calming my frazzled nerves. I fucking hate being hot. After four deployments and various other missions in the Middle East, I can't shake the automatic tension that builds, ready to snap, in a hot room. I was one of the lucky ones who came back whole, but I can't untrain my mind and body to realize I'm not in a war zone when my body temperature spikes.

I scan the back of the building and our surroundings. Randi steps out of my reach, settling on a stack of plastic crates someone stacked together in a makeshift seat. The scratch of flint meets my ears in the otherwise silent alley. With it being dinnertime, all the employees must be inside hard at work, preparing various meals for the hotel guests. Hopefully she'll be done with this smoke break before a lull allows their own breaks. The fewer people out here the better.

"So." After one more scan up and down the alley, I turn my attention to her. "You bring those bottles or what?" she asks as a puff of gray smoke billows from her lips. Smoking really shouldn't be as sexy as she's making it.

Instead of answering, I take the few steps toward her. The silk lining of my pocket slides across my knuckles as I grasp the two bottles and pull them free. Careful to not make the same mistake again, I drop the bottle in her awaiting hand, preventing any accidental skin-to-skin contact.

I watch in fascination as she bites the end of the lit cigarette, allowing it to dangle from her mouth, to open the tequila bottle with both hands.

"Who are you?" I ask before I can think better of it. At every turn, she's shocking me off my feet, completely disrupting everything I thought I knew about her. Hell, about women in general.

"No one. Haven't you figured that out yet?" Anger and concern strangle my chest at the sadness in her voice. "Right place, right time. Lucky. Whore. Gold digger. Fraud." Hazel eyes stare into my own. "Right?"

Well, that solidifies one thing I've always thought was debatable.

I *am* a complete ass.

CHAPTER FOURTEEN

RANDI

The smoke burns in my lungs oh so good. Damn, I missed this. The gum and other shit I've tried isn't the same. Something about being outside, the smoke-filled inhales and exhales combined with the delicious burn stall my constant thoughts. This right here, these few minutes, I get to relax. It's few and far between on the campaign trail, and I cherish each second of calm I can steal.

"I'm an ass," Trouble finally says. Twisting my lips, I blow smoke out the side of my mouth to keep from sending it into his face. "I didn't... I thought I knew you."

"You didn't. You don't." The glass rim of the bottle, still warm from his body heat, slips between my lips as I take a sip. "It's okay though. I'm still trying to figure out who I am, so I can't expect anyone else to figure it out before I do, you know." I let the comfortable silence fill the calm space between us before I go on. "But I can guarantee what you see is what you get. I've always been me and have fought to accept who I am, hot mess and all." I smirk using his words to describe me. It really is a perfect description of this life I find myself living.

I look up at the clink of glass on glass.

"Cheers to you being a hot mess and me being an ass, then."

Trouble tilts the bottle back, sucking down the entire contents. His

Adam's apple bobs with each deep swallow. I stare transfixed at the way it slides up and down tempting me to lean closer and take a nip.

"So, now that you know I'm not who you thought I was... friends?" My pitch rises with each word. I should be embarrassed by how bad I want him to say yes, but I'm not. I'm desperate in more ways than one. If I can trust him, trust Terminator and the rest of the team, maybe I have a sliver of a hope of surviving the next few months until the general election. After... well, let's just take it one step at a time.

"I have a friend."

"Oh, okay." The slow sip of tequila slides down my throat. "But do you want another one?"

Trouble's assessing gaze swipes up and down the alley. "Depends."

"On?"

"You. What's your angle?"

I tilt my chin higher to get a better look at his face. Not a single emotion displays across his features.

"My angle?" Leaning forward, I rest both elbows on my thighs. "Whoever hurt you worked you over good. Believe me, I've seen it, been there. If you're still this raw over it, I'm guessing it was recent."

His lips purse, flattening into a thin line.

"Right, you don't want to talk about it. That's cool, I get it. But to answer your question, I don't have an angle. Well...." I sigh and straighten my spine. "That's not true. I do have an angle, but it's not a bad one."

"What is it?" If I'm not mistaken, a hint of curiosity lines his voice.

"I need a friend, okay? I don't have anyone in DC I can trust. It's fucking lonely."

Those light brown eyes stop scanning for threats to meet mine. His brows furrow, forming a deep line between them. "You think you can trust me?"

Tapping the crates with the back of my heels, I shrug. "Yeah, I do, even though you're an ass."

He smirks at my words. "Trust is dangerous in politics." Thumb between my teeth, I chew on the ragged nail, waiting for him to continue. "Friends. I can do that."

I release the breath I was holding in a whoosh.

"Thank fuck."

"But we're not braiding each other's hair—"

"Obviously. You don't look like you'd be good at it. No offense."

"And the second I think you're fucking me over, we're done." He extends a hand between us. "Trey Benson. Pleased to meet you, friend."

I slide my own hand against his callused one. "Randi Sawyer. Nice to meet you, friend."

"Tell me your story," he says, crossing his arms over his chest. The buttons of his light blue dress shirt pull under the pressure. "From trailer to vying for the vice president spot. Must be a good one."

I snort and take a sip of tequila. The earlier bottle already warms my belly and loosens my normal hindrances of talking about my past.

"You saw where I grew up, and until Taeler was born, I thought Mom's life was my predestined future. But when I found out I was pregnant, and even more so after she was born, I wanted more for her, more for me. At that point, everything was spiraling out of control. Mom didn't want a baby interrupting her and her boyfriend's alone time, so she kicked me out to the shed." Memories flood my mind of the makeshift room slash nursery I created in the old storage shed. An unstoppable shudder shakes my body. Which of course he notices with those all-seeing eyes. "That didn't last long though. Taeler's dad's family stepped in, and... well, that's a whole different story that I don't want to get into."

My eyes widen, brows rising in question when he snags the cigarette box from my lap and lights up.

"Don't look so surprised. I don't know a single person who left the military without some kind of nicotine addiction."

"You're a veteran?" Of course he is. Bet you he looks hot as hell in whatever uniform he used to wear. Wonder if he still has it stashed somewhere.

"I am."

"Which branch?"

"Army."

I nod and light another cigarette. "A lot of the guys from my high school went in after graduation. Not a lot of choices unless you got an academic or sports scholarship for college. I was proud of them. I could never be that brave."

"Most of the boys under my command were the same. So fucking young."

"Oh," I say with an exhale of smoke. "Of course you were an officer." So hot.

"What made you go to UT and then law school? And not just any law school but Harvard?"

I roll the butt of the cigarette along my lower lip as I debate my response. "Someone told me I'd never amount to anything. That I'd never be more than an addict's daughter and would live the rest of my life in that same run-down trailer park. I wanted so badly to show them all they were wrong."

"I'd say you did."

I shake my head and swing my legs back and forth, kicking my heels against the thick plastic crates. "Not at first. When I first came home from law school, I did end up right back in the same trailer park, still broke, and even worse, in serious debt. I could've taken a job in Dallas, but I wanted to be close to Taeler. I'd already missed so much of her life, and I didn't want to miss any more."

"What happened?" he asks, taking a step closer. My shoulder brushes against his arm. The heat radiating off him begs me to inch closer. Of course I forgot my jacket upstairs. A strong, crisp fall breeze rips through the alley, racking my shoulders with a deep chill. Sealing the lit cigarette between his lips, Trey shrugs out of his suit jacket and drapes it across my shoulders.

"Thanks." I tug the two sides together making a makeshift cocoon with his jacket. I inhale deep, relishing in the faint scent of him. "What do you mean, what happened?"

"From being back in that small town with a law degree to running for vice president with dipshit Birmingham."

"Ah, that." *Tell the truth or the story we spun for the campaign. I can trust him; we are best friends, after all.* "The short version is I ruined his plans for world domination. I'm in over my head though and not really sure of my next move."

I glance up, fully expecting him to have more questions about my relationship with Kyle, but find him frowning at something down the alley.

"Ruined his plan?" I smile when his warm hand slides into mine. With a sharp tug, he yanks me from the stack of crates, causing them to tumble backward. "I need the full version not the short. But first...." Only after lighting up and taking a deep inhale does he motion for me to start. "Now I'm ready."

"So that's where we are," I say before taking another large bite from the juiciest double cheeseburger I've ever had. Do I feel bad taking Tank's cheeseburger and making him eat the tiny salad he ordered me? Not one bit. Rule number one, like he and I already covered, if you don't know, ask. If he would've, then he wouldn't be frowning over a plate of rabbit food right now.

Outside, I covered the basics on how Kyle approached me to be his wife before Trey cut me off, saying it would be best to head back upstairs to eat and let T hear everything too. Now they're *both* caught up on everything from the cover story to Kyle's harassment and Shawn's less-than-subtle threats.

"So, you're not with Birmingham?" Trey asks, disbelief in his tone. He hasn't stopped pacing since we got back up to the room. There's an ease in the way he moves, one fluid motion. Bet he'd be good in bed, fast and to the point. He doesn't come off as the cuddling type—another check in the win column for Trouble.

My eyes drop low, sliding down his body, pausing on his crotch.

"Randi."

I jump, somehow holding back a squeak of surprise. My gaze falls to the carpet in guilt. There's a slim chance he didn't notice me focused on his package. Peering through my dark lashes, I catch Trey's signature sexy smirk and divert my gaze anywhere other than him.

Shit. Busted.

I clear my throat and raise the burger, bringing it close to my lips. "What was the question again?"

"Are you fucking him?"

"Wow, so blunt. And no. Ew. Not that he hasn't tried, the depraved prick." T and Trey exchange a look. "What?" I ask before sinking my teeth into the cheeseburger.

I moan as I chew. Delicious.

"Birmingham said something different," T says, stroking his bald head. "Last night when he came by your condo."

I sort through all the possible reasons he'd do that while I finish chewing the large bite. "He was peeing on me."

"The fuck?" Trey says with a disgusted flinch.

"Not like that. Gross! What kind of shit are you into if that's where your mind goes, hmm?" I waggle a finger in Trey's direction and tsk. "Dirty mind. No, I mean he was marking his territory. But why? Why would Kyle want to keep you guys away from me?"

Trey clears his throat and pauses his pacing. Back against the far wall, he stuffs his large hands into the pockets of his suit. Two undone buttons of the crisp dress shirt pull with the movement, exposing a hint of chest. Why must he look like a mischievous male model? What stupid god did I piss off in life for them to dangle this untouchable hottie in my face?

It's mean. Wonder if there's a Secret Service suggestion box where I can file a 'please don't hire hotties' request so I'm not tempted on a second by second basis by a man I can't have. I should look into that.

"You with us, Randi?" T's deep voice pulls me out of my random thoughts.

"Yes. Of course I am. Well, maybe... actually, that's a hard no." I shrug and take another bite. I wink at T's glare as I chew. "It's really good. Thanks."

"You and my wife, taking my good food and replacing it with stuff fit for animals."

"I said," Trey interrupts, "before you got lost in your head—"

"It happens a lot. Get used to it."

"I grew up with Birmingham and Whit. Most of the fucksticks in DC, actually."

I nod, then shake my head. "Still though, why feel the need to pee on me?"

"Please stop saying that," Trey says on a sigh. I can't help but smile at his restrained annoyance. "Birmingham and I, plus Whit, have a rocky past."

"Ah, so it's less about me and more about you and Kyle." Mouth open, prepared to take another bite, I pause. "Wait. Oh hell, are you gay? Did y'all break up or something?"

"What the—"

"Now the bitter attitude makes sense. You were jealous, thinking I was sleeping with your ex–boyfriend."

Trey races closer, leaping over the coffee table. I shriek in excitement, the half-eaten burger falling forgotten to the plate. He grips the back of the couch on either side of my head, boxing me between his arms. In slow motion, he leans closer, and I sink deeper into the couch in retreat.

Deep, labored pants fan my face as he hovers inches from my face.

"Benson. Stop your shit. She didn't mean it," T calls out from somewhere in the distance, zero concern in his distracted tone.

"Take it back, or you'll regret it," Trey grunts, his almost smile taking the heat from his words.

"Are you a giver or a taker?" I say around a stifled giggle. Holy hell, it's hot in here. "I knew you were too pretty to be straight."

"There are twenty different ways I could kill you right now. I'm fucking badass, not pretty."

"Why does that turn me on?" His eyes widen at my breathy words. My chest rises and falls in quick succession, my pulse racing through my body, heating every inch. "There is something *seriously* wrong with me."

That damn sexy, mischievous smirk tugs at his edible lips. "Or very right." My breaths come in short pants. His lips brush against the shell of my ear, and I shiver at his raspy low voice. "I'm not gay, but I do love fucking a woman's nice round ass."

Who's wheezing? Shit. Am I wheezing? I'm wheezing.

What the hell? Sweat slicks my hands. At some point, my stomach slid up my throat and is now lodged there, preventing me from swallowing all the saliva building in my mouth.

"Get off her," T says, his words muffled like he's...

Tearing my lust-filled eyes from Trey's, I catch T as he shoves the last of the cheeseburger into his mouth.

"Hey." I pout. "That was mine." My hand vibrates with Trey's laugh as I shove against his chest to sit up.

T's broad shoulders rise and fall in an exaggerated shrug. "You dropped it, five second rule. Now back to business." The repetitive drumming of his fingers along the side table is the only sound in the quiet suite. Earlier Trey kicked the other agents out so I could tell the story without untrustworthy ears listening. "I'm guessing what happened last night with the accident somehow has to do with Shawn. I'll work on that angle once we get back to DC. It's good you told us; we can better protect you from inside threats now that we know to expect them."

"Great," I say with a yawn. A quick glance to the grandfather clock —because what hotel room doesn't have one of those—tells me it's just past ten. "As much fun as this has been, I have a shit ton of information to memorize before we head home tomorrow." The room spins a fraction as I stand. A hand dips beneath the suit coat I'm still wearing to slide around my waist, steadying me. I tip my head up. "Thank you."

"What are friends for?" A full, genuine smile spreads up Trey's cheeks. For a second, I stay mesmerized by the change in his face. The smirk is sexy, yes, but this smile? Hot fucking damn. The lightness in his features, the happiness in those bunched cheeks, gives him a fun-loving, boyish look.

"You should smile more," I whisper, still staring. I want that happy. The carefree, self-assured rightness in my life.

Soon. Even though money isn't an issue anymore, the pressure to keep proving myself is still there. Too many people still doubt me, hoping I fail. Once I prove everyone how wrong they are, how wrong they've been my whole life, maybe then I can be truly happy.

"Nah." He tugs, drawing me closer. "Come on. I'll help you to your room."

Each step forces our bodies to brush, shock waves of awareness from my racing heart zapping me with each accidental touch. As subtle as I can, I dip my nose to the coat still cocooning me in its warmth. His unique spicy scent fills my nose. As I take another long sniff, the stress from the last few hours eases from my shoulders, allowing them to drop from their place at my ears.

We pause halfway into the room. The fingers wrapped around my waist tighten.

"Where do you want to sit? Bed or chair?"

"Chair," I say, pointing to the plush chair I sat in earlier. "Shoot, I need my laptop bag." I try to shrug out of his hold, but his grip tightens, preventing me.

"I'll get it. You go get comfortable."

My gaze follows him until he disappears into the living room.

I only make it a few steps toward the chair when Trouble marches back in, annoyance written across his tight features. "Your phone's vibrating." It lands on the fluffy duvet with a poof. Reaching over, I flip it to check who it is.

'Blocked Caller' flashes on the black screen.

Kyle.

I swipe to answer and press it to my ear.

"Where are you?" he demands, forgoing any niceties.

"Dallas." The mattress presses against my backside as I perch on the edge. Leaning back on an elbow, I let my head fall back. "Things are taken care of with my mom. I'm looking into some exclusive rehab centers that promise confidentiality."

"I don't give a fuck what you're doing with her. Get your ass back to DC now."

My elbow slides along the soft fabric as I fall back onto the bed. "A lot has happened in the last twenty-four hours. I need some time to—"

"This isn't about you, Walmart, or have you not fucking figured that out yet? This is about winning and doing whatever I need you to do to ensure that we do. Get back on that jet right now. I need you in New York City Friday night to meet with a campaign donor. He wants to meet you."

"Well, that's promising. Maybe he likes my platform for lower taxes on the working—"

"That's not what he likes, you idiot. Damn, you're ignorant. Get your ass back here now so we can go over what I need you to do when you meet with him."

'Kyle, I don't feel comfortable—" I peel the hot glass from my ear and frown at the dark screen. Staring at the ceiling, I hold the phone to my chest.

"What was that about?" Trey's concerned face peers over the bed, blocking my view of the ceiling.

I roll my head back and forth. "We need to pack up and get back to DC tonight."

A heavy hand rests on the crown of my head. "What don't you feel comfortable with, Randi? What did that dipshit tell you to do?"

"Does it matter?" I slide my gaze to focus on his shoulder.

"Hey, look at me. Friends, right?"

I nod and bite my lower lip to keep it from trembling.

"Then what? Tell me."

"He wants me in New York to meet with a campaign donor. I get the impression the guy has other things than discussing the campaign on the agenda."

Trouble curses. The bed dips, making me roll toward the middle, my side smooshing up against his thigh. Pressing my cheek against the duvet, I stare up at his profile. He's propped on the edge of the bed, his head tipped back, eyes focused on the ceiling.

"Don't do it." A hunk of dark hair slides across his forehead as pleading eyes meet mine. "I have zero right to tell you what to do, but don't do it."

"I don't have a choice," I whisper. The fear of returning home, once again unsuccessful in life, lodges in my throat. "I can't go home. Can't go back to living like that day after day."

"You always have a choice."

"Easy for you to say. You don't have as much to lose as I do."

"Don't I?" he grits out. "I have more on the table than you realize. Don't judge me when you get pissed that people do the exact same to you."

My lashes flutter closed. "You're right. But it doesn't change the situation or the outcome."

"Fight back. Be a fighter in this. Don't give in to his demands sitting down."

The determination in his voice, in the stern look on his face, urges me to listen. Digging my elbows into the duvet, I lean forward and knock his bicep with my shoulder. "Okay, Yoda. How do you propose I fight this when I have zero leverage?"

My heart thunders against my chest as one corner of his lip tugs up. "I have a few ideas."

Excitement and unease swirl in my belly like a group of butterflies all taking flight at the same time.

Maybe I am as crazy as people think I am, because I'm smiling right back.

CHAPTER FIFTEEN

RANDI

R ivers of rain stream down the town car's window, the stoplight above highlighting their path with a bright red backdrop. Elbow on the armrest of the door, I sigh, a patch of condensation appearing atop the dark glass from my breath.

New York City. I would be excited if it weren't for the crazy nerves hijacking my emotions.

A warm palm slides over my bare knee. I shift my observing eyes from the passing umbrellas lining the sidewalks to the contact.

Fine lines, some from age and some from injuries leaving faint white scars, mar Trey's tan hand. A simple swipe of his thumb along the inside of my knee sends a chill racing through my veins, having nothing to do with the cool temperature inside the car. I swallow back the building unease, my gaze shifting from his hand to the man himself.

"We'll be with you every step of the way," Trey says, his tone low, soothing. "If you want to cancel—"

I give him an adamant shake of my head. Peering through the darkness, I meet his concerned brown eyes. "No, I have to do this. You know I do. This is my chance to gain leverage on those assholes. It's a great plan."

"Some might even call it brilliant."

A snort tickles my nose. The expensive fabric of my cocktail dress slides along the soft leather of the seat as I adjust, angling my knees toward Trey, who sits inches away in the other passenger seat. "I'll call it brilliant if it works."

All humor leaves his face. His eyes shift, and I track the path of his gaze to where his hand still rests on my knee, that sneaky thumb still swiping along my bare skin.

He pulls his hand away, the heat that was building between my thighs following suit.

He clears his throat. "Sorry."

I bite the tip of my tongue to keep myself from begging him to move it back. His touch, the soft yet powerful way his skin feels against mine, is more than welcomed. Not sure what that means, but for the first time in my life, I want a comforting caress from someone besides Taeler. His comforting yet possessive hands holding me close.

In the back seat of the sleek black town car, I meet his intense stare as the passing streetlights filter in and out through the windows. It's only been a few days since we met, but there's something building between us. Something deeper than I've experienced even with people I've known for years. He sees me, the real me. And I see bits of the real Trey Benson. I see the slivers he doesn't intentionally show. The soft touches, considerate actions, and supportive words.

And I want more.

Want it all.

"Almost there," T says from the driver seat. I reluctantly pull my gaze from Trey's to glance out the windshield. The wipers swipe back and forth in slow repetitive arcs. "I still don't like it."

I bite back a smile. Of course the cautious and careful Terminator doesn't like this crazy plan. To be honest, I'm not a huge fan either, but it's the perfect scenario to kill three birds with one stone. If it works.

No, it will work.

My chest pitches forward as we slide to a stop in front of a dazzling hotel. The brilliant blue lights cast a strange hue over T and Gremlin.

I inhale deep, filling my lungs with the determination and strength to get through this night and finally, *finally* have the upper hand in life. The leather groans beneath my backside as I rotate toward the door, waiting for the approaching bellhop to pull it open.

"Randi?" I turn my chin, glancing over my shoulder to T. "If you feel this won't work, or if you're scared or... anything, get out. Give the code word and it's done whether we have the information we need or not. Got it?"

My dark hair slides forward across my shoulder at my tight nod.

"What's the code word again?" he demands.

"Pumpkin spice latte," I say with a grin. That was T's addition to the plan. I wanted 'sparkle the unicorn' as the code word, but neither him nor Trey thought I could find a way to work it into a normal sentence. Just proves they don't know me as well as they think they do.

A burst of cool, damp air brushes against my legs and floats a few sections of hair across my face. I face the familiar callused palm dangling midair, waiting for my own. With another deep breath, I slide my fingers between Trey's and wrap my fingers around his own. I fold out of the car, stepping cautiously onto the sidewalk in my heels. I glide both hands down the thick material of my black dress, repositioning the hem from where it rode up my thighs.

Tipping my chin, I take a step toward the enormous revolving doors. Sweat beads along my palms the closer we get. Rapid breaths steal the air from my lungs, making my head fuzzy.

"Calm down," Trey says. I flick an annoyed glance his way at the laughter in his tone. "You're fine."

A tight smile pulls at my lips for Gremlin, who holds the side door open for us, as we step into the hotel lobby.

All the building anxiety melts away as Trey presses his hand against the small of my back. Slowing my pace to increase the comforting pressure, I give my fingers a tiny shake. My heels click along the polished marble as we stride across the lobby toward the restaurant where I'm meeting the campaign donor.

The plan is simple: gain information we can use to blackmail him and get out. The information can be anything from bribery all the way to harassment. Whatever it ends up being, I hope it happens fast. The less time I have to spend with this guy the better. Being alone with him isn't on my top twenty things to do while in New York City.

"I wish I could see the city," I say to Trey, my attention staying on the approaching hostess stand. Mr. Hindle, the campaign donor, insisted we meet here. The fact that it's a restaurant inside this upscale hotel didn't pass my notice. "I've only been here for rallies or something else to do with the campaign. Never seen the city like a real tourist."

The pressure on my back changes as he guides me through the intimate tables of the restaurant. I scan the large area over the packed crowd for the man I'm meeting.

"Back booth. More secure," Trouble whispers into my ear. "Almost there. You good? Head in the game?"

No. "Yes."

We don't say another word. The restaurant darkens the farther back we go, the other patrons' murmurs growing quieter. An older man slides from a small intimate booth. I recognize him immediately based off the pictures and information Kyle had me review in DC. Early sixties, multimillionaire, wants world domination. Okay, that's not one hundred percent true. In exchange for funneling millions into our campaign fund, he wants a blind eye on his companies unfavorable working conditions if we win.

I shudder at the way his clouded eyes ogle my thin frame. Not as thin as it was last year before I met Kyle but still putting on weight in the right areas has been a challenge. The hand at my back tightens to a fist, the knuckles now digging into my lower spine. I chance a peek up to Trouble, but he doesn't notice. His intense stare is locked on the donor with a promise of a slow death behind those honey brown eyes. I love the humor and twinkle I normally see, the side he shows me, but this side of Trouble is just as sexy.

That intensity, the utter control the man exudes, zaps the final drop of worry clouding my thoughts. He's here. T's outside. Gremlin and the rest of the boys are waiting in the shadows.

I can do this. They're trusting me to have the balls to get through this, and I will not let them down.

They believe in me. It's time I did too.

"Miss Sawyer." Mr. Hindle leans forward, pressing a swift kiss to one cheek, then the other. "Thank you for meeting me."

"The pleasure is mine," I say, somehow suppressing my utter disdain from seeping through.

He raises his hand to the side, extending into the booth. I swallow hard and step out of Trouble's comforting touch. The dress's hem rides up my thighs as I slide along the supple leather semicircle booth. Settled on the opposite side, Mr. Hindle climbs in and keeps going, pausing when our knees touch but keeping a respectable distance between us for the world to see. Sneaky prick. I grip the hem of my dress beneath the crisp white table linen and give it a quick tug as I cross one leg over the other, sealing my thighs tightly together.

"You can leave."

My mouth pops open. Attention flying from the front of my dress to Mr. Hindle, I shift back against the tufted black leather of the booth at his pinched features. But his annoyance isn't directed to me. My gaze floats across the table in the direction of Mr. Hindle's glare. My own eyes widen in surprise.

Trey still stands at the booth opening. Stance wide, hands lightly folded in front, exuding refined power. Not money power like the filthy idiot beside me. No, real power. The kind of energy that radiates off someone who knows without a doubt he or she can handle whatever comes their way.

"My team is conducting one more sweep of the restaurant as we speak. I'll move as soon as I get the all clear."

If Mr. Hindle doesn't catch the unspoken 'asshole' at the end, I'll be shocked.

Several tense seconds tick by while the two men battle for dominance.

"All clear." Trouble's eyes flick to me. My breath catches knowing this means he's leaving me here alone. "Ma'am."

I watch as he turns and fades into the dark corners of the restaurant where no doubt the rest of the team is waiting.

My foot taps furiously in the air beneath the table.

I'm up.

Careful to keep my movements smooth, I slide my red clutch from where it rests on the seat to the table. It's not super close to Mr. Hindle, but T assures me the tiny listening device tucked in the pocket will pick up our conversation just fine as long as it's within reach. I tug it a bit closer just in case.

Hands fidgeting, nerves at an all-time high, I adjust and readjust the five forks and thirty spoons surrounding the single white plate to give my anxious fingers something to do while Mr. Hinkle smiles seeming to enjoy my uncomfortableness.

A stiff back waiter approaches with zero animation on his surly face. Without asking what I would like, Mr. Hindle immediately speaks up to order an expensive bottle of red wine and waves the waiter off with an arrogant flick of the wrist.

"How's DC treating you?" he asks after the waiter scurries away.

I roll my shoulders and adjust in the booth.

Game time.

"Different than Texas, that's for sure. Complex, fast paced, brilliant are a few words I'd use to describe what I've seen so far."

He chuckles and rests a wrinkled hand on top my own. He gives a pointed look to their constant movement. "First time doing this?"

"This?" Oh, please tell me he's going to say something sleazy so I can get the hell out of here sooner than later.

"Meeting with a campaign donor, of course." His easy chuckle rakes my frayed nerves. "Let's get some wine in us before we dive into the business side, shall we? I have to admit your background is intriguing to me."

"Oh?" I move my hand from under his, tucking it in my lap. "And why's that?"

"It's different. Most of the people in this town don't know what it's like to live below the 1 percent. Hearing your perspective through the campaign coverage so far has piqued my interest. Tell me a bit about yourself, Randi. Can I call you Randi?"

I force a stiff nod. "There isn't much to tell, but you're correct that my perspective is different. I know what it's like to scrape by, to have your hard-earned money be siphoned away before you even can cash your paycheck."

"And that's what you want to change. I like that. Tell me more."

The tight tension in my gut fades. My shoulders relax and my foot stops its midair thumping. Maybe Kyle was wrong about what this guy wants from me. He's pitched forward, elbows on the table, fully engaged in what I have to say. Embarrassed warmth sparks along my cheeks, no doubt turning them a bright pink. What if all this was for nothing and this guy is just a nice old man?

As the waiter holds out the bottle for Mr. Hindle's inspection, I detail out my thoughts and ideas on how to change the lives of those who fall beneath the middle-class financial status. By the time I wrap up my crazy ideas—Kyle's words, not mine—excitement flickers in my belly and hope flows through my veins, making my fingers twitch in anticipation. If I can get this man to see things from my point of view, maybe Kyle will change his tune and let me spearhead some of these projects.

A wide smile stretching across my face, I lean forward, reaching for my wineglass, only to find it empty. Huh, when did that happen?

"It's good, isn't it? At four hundred dollars a bottle, it should be." My fingers slip from the glass. I shift my gaze to his—still full. "I'll get you another bottle."

Another?

Frantic, I glance around the restaurant, but with the lights dimmed and zero windows, there's nothing to use to judge how much time as passed during my long-winded rant.

"Sorry, I-I got carried away," I stutter. Condensation slicks my palm and fingers as I grasp the water glass and lift it to my lips.

"No need to be embarrassed, Randi." The seat shifts my weight, angling me toward Mr. Hindle as he scoots an inch closer. My muscles tense at the brush of his suit pants along the skin of my bare thigh.

My breath hitches.

Kyle was right, I am an idiot. I played right into this fucker's hands.

At the first brush of his fingers along my knee, I jerk out of his reach.

"Come on now, Randi, don't be that way." This time his fingers clamp around my exposed thigh, preventing me from flinching away. "I can do so much for your cause."

"If...?" I ask, not having to add a tremble to my tone. It's already there.

"I think that's something we can discuss after dinner, don't you?"

No. I can't let it get that far. If I go up to his room, like I'm sure he'll suggest, I'm done for. He's twice my size; if he tries anything, there's no way I could fight him off. Plus, behind closed doors, I won't have Trey's hawk eyes monitoring the situation.

This needs to end now, even though he's not lying about the wine. That shit is yummy with a capital Y. I'd take a picture of the label to buy later, but even if I had enough money to wipe my ass with hundred-dollar bills, I couldn't justify spending that kind of cash on a single bottle of wine.

Case? Debatable. But bottle, no way. Do you know how many boxes of wine you could buy for four hundred dollars? A lot, that's how much.

His soft skin slides up toward the juncture of my legs that's securely sealed off by the closed thighs, pulling me back to the present.

"I know how much this means to you," he mutters. "Have you found a rehab center for your mother yet?"

The sip of water I just took sputters back into my glass. "What?" I say on a deep cough, trying to clear the rest of the water from my lungs and give me a moment to wrap my head around his words. "How did you—"

"Enough money in the right hands and you can find the truth in anything." I balk at his cold sneer. "You see, Randi, this is in your best interest. We can make a deal, you and I."

"And what deal is that?"

"Eager," he says, digging his fingers deeper into my flesh. I hide my wince of pain behind the water glass at my lips. "I like that."

"What do you want, Mr. Hindle?" I straighten my spine. I will not bow to this fucker. "I thought this was about your business and your donation to the campaign."

"Ah, that. Kyle and I already discussed the terms."

"What?" I gasp.

"You didn't know?" He releases my thigh. Immediately I move out of his reach, sliding to the other side of the booth. "Figures he wouldn't fill you in."

"In on what?" I grit out. Fuck Kyle and his power moves. Moving me around the country like his little pawn protecting the damn king.

"You sealing the deal, of course."

I slump forward, all fight draining from my muscles.

"Don't look so repulsed. I'm not that bad, am I?"

I school my features, keeping the hint of excitement from showing. *This* is my opening.

"Depends," I say in the meekest tone I can muster. "What... what do you want from me? I don't understand what you're referring to."

"You want me to spell it out for you, sweetheart?"

I fight a cringe.

Fluttering my lashes, I glance around the restaurant, pretending to ensure no one is around. I moisten my lower lip with a slow swipe of my tongue. "Yes."

His cold eyes fall to my wet lip as he licks his own in anticipation. I battle internally to not shudder in disgust. "Come to my room and I'll show you."

Well hell. Maybe a different angle?

"If I do this, if I come up to your room, you'll keep my mom out of this? You'll give the money to the campaign?"

"We can work out the terms upstairs, but yes, in a nutshell. Give me what I want, and I'll make sure the money is deposited tomorrow."

Rallying what bit of courage I have left, I scoot along the booth, our hips now touching. "So how does this work? A promise of a hundred grand for you to fuck my mouth? Five hundred for me to spread my legs?"

His eyes darken with lust, beads of sweat glistening across his creased brow.

This is where I want him. On the edge of reason, tipping over into the abyss of dark desire.

"And how much for my ass?" I whisper into his ear. Ugh, I'll need two scalding showers to remove the ick from my skin. "How much is my entire body worth to you?"

"Two million." His voice is coarse with the gallons of desire pumping through his veins. "Two million dollars to the campaign if you let me pound into your ass." His rapid, hot breaths brush over my face as he leans close. "Another million, and my promise to keep your family's finances out of the press, if you make that arrogant agent watch."

Fucking creeper.

I open my mouth to tell him just as much but gasp at the panic in Mr. Hindle's bulging eyes. The leather slips beneath my sweaty palms as I scramble down the booth.

Trey sits on the opposite side of Mr. Hindle, their shoulders close enough to touch.

"You want me to watch, do you?" Trey's arm beneath the table shifts, and Mr. Hindle gasps, face paling. The hate threatening behind Trey's light eyes disappears when his gaze shifts to me. "I think we got enough, don't you?"

Mr. Hindle's narrowed eyes flick between me and Trouble. "You set me up." Red clutch in hand, I raise it in the air. His clouded eyes search the bag like he's scanning the recording itself, replaying every word he said tonight. "Nothing will hold up in court. You've got nothing, you fucking conniving—" A sharp whistle of air cuts off his words as he sucks in a quick breath.

What in the hell is Trey doing under the table? I tilt my head in question, but he shakes his. Hmm, he'll tell me later, then.

I shift my focus back to the sweaty Mr. Hindle. The air of power and influence is gone, his older age showing as his skin pales.

"You're correct, nothing will hold up in court." His brows rise and a flush of life spreads back into his gaunt face. "But that wasn't what I was going for. You see, I've noticed that in today's social media society, justice doesn't mean anything. One slip of the voice recording leaked on the internet, one accusation, and poof, someone is guilty in everyone's opinion before the case ever sees a courtroom. Trial by Twitter. It's a thing." His shoulders round as the truth in my words sink in. "Do you care what the public thinks of you? What about that beautiful young wife of yours? Oh, and your five kids. What would they think if they heard daddy dearest demanding sexual favors in exchange for money?" I click my tongue and tilt my head. "And the watching part? That's dark."

"What do you want?" he bites out, holding as still as a statue.

Seriously, does Trey have this guy's balls in a vise or something? I fight the urge to dip under the table and see what the hell is going on under there.

"A few things, actually. First, I need you to tell Kyle everything went smoothly tonight and pay out whatever you agreed on." A blast of satisfaction fills every inch of my heart at the condemning look he shoots my way. Not sure why he's pissed at me; he's the old dirty bastard. "Second, you'll also tell him to keep his hands off me or you'll pull your donation."

"Why the fuck would I do that?"

I wave a hand in dismissal. "I don't know. Think of something. Maybe that you want me all to yourself or something. I don't care."

Seconds tick by, the murmuring of the other patrons, oblivious to what we're doing, filling the background. I lick my lower lip as I eye his still-full glass of wine. Would it be bad form to let that go to waste? I can't let down those poor grapes who lost their lives for this wine. Lifting one shoulder in agreement with my internal debate, I reach across the table and cradle the delicate glass in my palm.

"Seriously?" Trey admonishes.

I shrug and take a sip.

"For all this, you'll destroy the recording?"

I nod and pause, holding up a finger. "Also, no releasing my mom's information to the press. And if I ever hear you're attempting to extort sexual favors for political ones again, I'll release the recording and pay a visit to your wife personally to tell her everything that happened tonight. 'Kay? 'Kay."

I shouldn't wink. That would be an asshole move.

Eh.

I wink.

He begrudgingly grunts some form of acknowledgment. Good enough for me.

Another hasty sip. Yum, so good.

You know what? Fuck it. I slide my phone from the clutch and snap a picture of the bottle. Maybe it can be a special occasion bottle, like when the queen visits or I'm successful in securing world peace.

I scoot out of the booth to stand, skimming both palms down the black material, drying them and pushing the hem back down my thighs in one move. The dress is beautiful, classy yet sexy. Too bad I'll burn it after tonight. I don't care how much it cost; I could never wear it again without remembering this asshole's hands on me.

I'm held captivated with acute interest as Trey leans closer to Mr. Hindle, whispering something in his ear. I track Trey's movements as he shifts out of the booth and stands beside me. Our eyes meet, something dangerous and hot flaring between us.

I turn my attention back to the table, locking eyes with the slimy bastard.

"Nice doing business with you, Mr. Hindle. Thank you for the wine. It was delicious."

I spin from the table, more than ready to put this night behind me. My feet don't get a single step before a comforting hand presses against my lower back, guiding me through the restaurant once again.

I won this battle.

We won this battle.

One of many in this political warfare I've immersed myself in, I'm sure.

I glance over my shoulder to Trey, a smile spreading up my lips. At least I'm not alone.

CHAPTER SIXTEEN

TREY

Muscles tense, hands fisted, I fight the urge to turn and skewer that rat bastard's balls with the steak knife I left on the booth seat. The magic lessons as a kid come in handy at times; tonight was one of them. No one noticed the slight of hand as I swiped the seemingly unsuspecting knife from the table. No one except Mr. Hindle, who felt said knife slicing through his suit pants, readying to do the same to his sac if he so much as breathed too deep.

Tank set it up for the team to hear every word through the small listening device hidden in that tiny purse of hers. How I kept myself from tackling the fucker as he played Randi with the expensive wine and faking to be interested in the causes she holds close, I'll never know. I deserve a big fucking gold star next to my name.

The old fucker should be tortured and left for dead for even thinking it was okay to extort a woman like that. A snarl pulls at my face. I know from personal experience that he's just one of hundreds, if not thousands, in the corrupt political scene.

A forceful relieved exhale pushes from my chest as we exit the restaurant into the much cooler hotel lobby.

Instead of directing Randi toward the front doors where Tank and the other boys wait to whisk her back to the jet, I tug her close and divert us down a long hall.

"Um, Trouble, where—"

I press a finger to my lips, cutting her off. The clicking of her heels echoes down the empty hall, mine silent with each step. Searching right and then left, I grip her elbow and tug her toward a conference room door. I press an ear to the door and listen.

Nothing.

Perfect.

The door clicks open with ease, and I pull her through after me. Darkness engulfs the large ballroom except for the bright band of light cutting through its inky blackness from the hallway. I tip my face to meet hers, wide hazel eyes searching mine.

The door snaps closed, eliminating the last bit of light.

Darkness envelops us. A bolt of satisfaction shoots through my chest as her smaller body presses against my own. Without questioning the emotions spurring the moment, I wrap an arm around her shoulders, tucking her tighter against my chest. Here, she's safe. Away from the corrupt world that wants nothing more than to conquer and pillage her trusting soul. A growing part of me doesn't want her to win in the general election. She's too good for this town. I've seen what the political game does to women like her, seen the bitter shell left behind.

Through the earpiece, Tank demands our location.

"Tank, listen, man. Don't be mad." I wince at the explosion of curse words in my ear. "But we're going off-line for a little while. Don't worry, big guy, we'll be fine."

At that, I tug the earpiece from my ear and turn off the radio. Digging around my pants pocket, I pull out my phone and press the flashlight icon. Randi's sweet face pinches as she pulls back from the bright light assaulting her unprepared eyes.

"Do you or do you not want to see New York City while you're here?" Her eyes search mine before glancing to the closed door. "If you're ready to go back, then we walk out of here and head to the jet. I just thought after all that"—my muscles tighten, tugging her closer

—"you'd want a night off. You didn't get one in Dallas. This is your chance."

"What about the team?" she asks. I tug on her hand for her to release the thumbnail she's chewing on. "Can we go out there alone?"

"Do you trust me?" I ask, seriousness filling my voice. If she doesn't, hell, that'll be a blow I'm not prepared to take.

An eternity seems to pass between the moment my question leaves my lips and her answer. I want her to rely on me. No, I'm *desperate* for her to rely on me, to see me as her protector. A man who will fight to keep her safe from the DC wolves and threats to her life.

"Yes," she says with a smile. "Yes, I trust you."

My lips curl, mirroring her own. "Good. Then let's go."

"Wow," she says on a pushed breath.

Standing close, I peer down, soaking in her palpable excitement. Around us, lights blink throughout glittering Times Square. Thousands of tourists shuffle, bumping against each other, moving bodies like human bumper cars. Horns blare over the music pouring from various stores. In the center of the exciting madness, the Naked Cowboy strums away on his guitar, eating up the attention.

With her excitement, it's like seeing it all for the first time, even though it could easily be my hundredth. I chuckle in amusement as she points at the nearly naked man, her brows waggling suggestively beneath the "I Love NYC" hat pulled low.

The hat and sweat suit, plus the flip-flops—all her idea, not mine— were a necessary purchase after we broke out of the hotel's back exit, hightailing it down various streets to escape a murderous Tank.

I offered to buy her something less... well, ugly. That's the best way to put it. But she refused, saying the New York Yankees sweatpants and sweatshirt were perfect. Paired with a pair of gaudy flip-flops from another vendor and she's a hilarious hot mess. Not that she seems to care one bit. Hell, she didn't even bat an eye at having to change in a dark alley or the hot dog stand I suggested for dinner.

This woman tosses everything I know about women out the window and has ruined me for the Political Barbies in DC forever. This is fun. Easy. The last time I was in New York, all I saw was the inside of high-end boutiques and department stores as Rachel lit my credit card on fire. Thank fuck I didn't give in to her pouting when I wouldn't go into Harry Winston with her. The media circus around our breakup would've been ten times worse if there was a broken engagement tossed into the shit show.

I stumble at the insistent tug on my elbow. A lock of hair falls along my forehead as I shake my head in amusement. Randi leads us through the swarm of people, talking a thousand words a second over her shoulder as she points up at the bright billboards with the hand not pulling me along.

Maybe I should send Shawn a thank-you card for helping me see that Rachel and I were a forced fit. It sucked at the time, yes, and hell, it still does at night when I fall asleep horny and alone. My poor dick hasn't felt anything other than my own hand in way too long.

My gaze falls to Randi's round ass accentuated by the draping material of the soft sweatpants. At my back, someone stumbles in to me, shoving me forward. Our feet tangle, her loud gasp barely audible above the other noise on the street. I wrap both arms around her waist, lifting her off the sidewalk and tucking her close to my chest. A couple intentional steps forward and I'm once again steady on my feet. But still I don't drop her. Instead, I tug her closer, the crease of her ass cradling my hardening cock.

Fuck, she feels fantastic, and this is with clothes on.

Her chest expands and shrinks in rapid succession beneath my forearms.

Around us the crowd shuffles, ignoring our tight embrace. Oblivious to my internal battle to not fuck her against the nearest wall. The need to take her, to make her scream my name, increases every day we're together, every second more torturous than the last. I shouldn't want her. Not because of her background or her lack of wealth but because she's the job. My job is to protect her, keep her safe, and here I am unable to think beyond the way my dick feels pressed against her.

This is a terrible idea, but I can't stop. I don't want to stop.

I want her, all of her, every inch and every breath begging for me.

"Trey?" Wiggling in my hold, she rotates to dip her head back, hazel eyes finding mine.

"Randi."

"Um, I can't really, you know, breathe here."

Shit.

"Sorry," I grumble and ease my hold, savoring the slide of her body against mine. "You ready to get out of here? Head back?"

The excitement and joy falls from her face.

"Do we have to?" she asks, looking to the sidewalk. I stare at her hat-covered head, not understanding what just happened to flip her mood. "If you're worried about the crowd, we can go somewhere else." Pushing to her tiptoes, she looks right, left, over her shoulder, and then over mine, looking back down the street. "Where's Central Park?"

Reaching out, I interlace our fingers and meet her hopeful gaze. "Come on, Mess. It's this way."

With the hustle of the crowd behind us, I flex my fingers to release her hand, but hers tighten, keeping my hand clasped.

Okay then.

Stepping over a line, but that's okay. She probably needs to feel safe as we navigate the streets of New York City, and holding my hand like a drowning victim does a life preserver offers that sense of safety. I should not read into the simple gesture. Which I'm not, except my semi isn't listening, and it's fucking chafing the hell out of the tip.

"You seem like you've been here before," Randi says beside me. Her head is on a swivel, taking in every building and storefront.

"I have—several times, in fact—but I'll tell you something, Mess. It's a different experience with you."

I smirk at her responding snort. "Mess? Is that what you're calling me now?"

I shrug and look away so she doesn't catch my smile.

"I should be offended, yet it fits. I'll allow it. And you know you use that word a lot when you describe me."

"Mess?"

"No, different."

"Ah." I tug her to a stop to keep from being run over by a speeding taxi. "It's the best way I can describe it. It's a good thing though, so you know. It's... vibrant."

"Vibrant."

I shake my head. "It's hard to explain. I've seen the world through a certain lens for thirty-eight years, and then you come along and turn things from versions of gray to full of color. Full of life. I've never known someone who sees the world for what it is and not what they can get from it."

I glance down to gauge her reaction only to find her head down, the bill of the hat blocking her face from view. A quiet sniffle meets my listening ears. Another has me tugging her to a stop, but still she keeps her face down. Bending my knees, I lower a few inches, putting me at her level. Two fingers beneath her chin, I tilt her face to meet mine.

Well, fuck me.

Wet streaks glisten along her full cheeks in the overhead street-light. Unease at her red-rimmed eyes steals the air from my lungs.

Large tears roll down from the inside corner of both eyes. "That was the nicest... the nicest thing anyone has ev-ever said to me. About me. Thank you."

Talk about a knife to the heart. I ball my hands into tight fists as anger and resentment build, rolling together and growing larger and volatile. If that's the nicest thing anyone has ever said to her.... I shake my head. Nope, can't go there or I'll go on a killing streak, murdering everyone who's ever said an ill word toward her.

"You're breaking my heart here, Mess." I tug slightly on her hand until her chest is pressed against mine. Eyes to the sky, I mentally list the Redskins' roster, hoping to distract me from her squished tits rubbing against me.

I'm going through the 2018 lineup when she finally pulls back, wiping her nose with the sleeve of the sweatshirt.

"I'm okay, just didn't expect that, and after tonight with... you know. I'm just on edge. Then you go and say something nice, and here I am losing my shit on the streets of New York City." She takes another step back, fully pulling out of my embrace, and starts toward the park once again.

"Different circumstances, but I do know what it's like to not have support, or hell, even a positive word come out of your parent's mouth. How do you do it?" Hands in my pockets, I slow my steps to keep pace with hers. "Everything you've lived through, pushed through, yet you're still pushing forward, striving for more."

The tips of her fingers slide inside the sleeves of her sweatshirt before she tucks her arms around her chest. "Speaking of parents, thanks for the rehab referral. It's working out great so far. Costing me a kidney, but hopefully it makes a lasting impact this time."

"You're welcome. Glad I could help take some stress off."

"And to answer your question, I guess you can say me growing up the way I did made me positive instead of desolate. Everywhere around me I saw where giving up would get you, and I didn't want that. Not for me or for Taeler. So I stayed positive, kept that hope of a better life alive day after day, even when things were tight and I didn't want to stay strong. That's the thing about being a parent, you can't give up. You have someone looking up to you, counting on you to give them their best life. I couldn't give up because I couldn't give up on Taeler."

"You were fifteen when you felt that?"

She shrugs, dismissing the awe in my voice.

"Randi, most people don't realize that even when they become parents later in life. Our world is a selfish black hole that sucks your will to live—"

"You're kind of dramatic for a guy, you know that?"

A sense of relief floods through me at the smile in her voice. "All I'm saying is you're special. Don't ever forget that. Whether you win or lose in November, always remember there is no one like you out there in this world, and anyone who takes the time to get to know you, the real you, is lucky as hell."

CHAPTER SEVENTEEN

RANDI

The night air turns crisp, any warmth from the day gone as we walk and talk through the nearly deserted park. Trey turned off our cell phones and the listening device before leaving the hotel to prevent T from tracking us, and the freedom from the stupid electric device is amazing. You don't realize the disservice the constant connection to the outside world is until its leash is severed and you're freed.

"I hope I get to meet her," Trey says. He hasn't wandered but a few inches from my side since we left the hotel. He stays close to keep me safe, but I can't help the building hope that it's more than protection keeping him there.

The desperate need to touch him, to feel his body against mine was merciless when we first met, but that was simple attraction. Now? Oh boy. Totally different ball game.

Not only is he attractive with his roguish good looks, but he's tough as nails when he needs to be, then comforting and sweet when he doesn't. And what he said earlier about me being bright and shit left my face and panties damp. I almost pulled the oversized sweat-pants down right there on the sidewalk and bent over. I chose not to since, you know, I don't want to come off as desperate or anything.

Which I totally am.

"Not tonight. I didn't shave."

"Huh?" He stumbles midstep and turns with a confused look. "Mess, I don't even want to know what line of thinking made you respond with that."

I cringe. "Sorry, wrong conversation again."

"I was referring to Taeler."

Oh, right. "You might, I guess. Depending if we win or not. I'm trying to keep her as far away from all this as possible. The DC crowd as a whole, but mostly Kyle and Shawn. I wouldn't put it past them to leverage her in some way to use me."

"Smart. You should consider sending her to Oxford. It's farther, and not in America."

"Not a bad plan, Trouble, but so far UT is working out great." With a content sigh, I try to commit this moment to memory. "The fall is so beautiful here. At home, the leaves don't change to these bright colors, or if they do, it only lasts a week before the wind strips them bare." Bending forward, I swipe a wet yellow leaf from the walkway. Thank goodness the rain stopped sometime during the blackmail mission, leaving behind only crisp, damp air and sporadic puddles to avoid. "You've asked a lot of questions about my life but haven't really given me much about yours."

"Not much to tell," he says with a shrug. "I live in DC now, college on the West Coast, army. Nothing exciting."

I tilt backward, almost toppling over at his arm shooting out, pressing against my stomach and stopping me in my tracks. My heart rate ratchets higher as he scans a block of darkened path up ahead with intense scrutiny. Goose bumps spread along my forearms. The darkness of the night mixed with our isolation urges me closer to Trey's side. He wraps his arm around my shoulders, tucking me even closer. An engulfing sense of security warms my chilled body like a thick blanket.

"What's going on?" I whisper, my lips brushing the material of his suit jacket.

"You feel that?" Head on a swivel, he scans the area once, twice.

A sudden prickling spreads down my neck at the sense of being watched.

"Let's go back the way we came."

I'm still nodding when he whirls us around to retrace our steps. My breath catches as every muscle of his that's pressed against my right side tenses. The silhouette outside a streetlight's illumination pulls us to a hard stop.

Trey swears under his breath. The world spins as he rotates us back around only to find another person, this one in the middle of the path, not caring that the light gives us a clear visual of his features.

"Mess," Trey states as he looks from the man in front of us to the one at our back. "I need you to stay close, but know when to get out of the way if things get dirty. You understand me?"

My head bobs in rapid succession.

"Dammit, I really didn't think this through, did I?"

The regret in his voice tugs at my heart. "Hey, you didn't know. Don't blame yourself."

"It's Central Park at midnight."

"Who knows? Maybe these guys just need directions." I push as much humor into my shaky voice as possible.

As we talk, the two men move closer, boxing us in.

"Wallet, watch, jewelry," one guy orders, his voice gruff.

"So that's a no to the directions," I say on a giggle. Shit, why am I laughing? What is wrong with me? "This is not funny." Another burst of giggles erupts from my chest. I smack both hands over my mouth. "Sorry," I mumble.

"You don't want to do this," Trey says, his voice hard, all business. "I'm not your normal tourist."

Peering around Trey's shoulder, I shrink against his side. "That one's getting closer," I whisper.

"They both are, Mess. It's okay."

Is it? From where I'm standing, nothing is okay. My legs tremble with the urge to run.

"Money, now," the one in front of us demands, more grit in his voice this time.

"That's a hard pass," Trey says. His muscles bunch, the arm around my shoulders sliding to my lower back. "Duck and crawl to the edge of the path." His words barely register before he gives my back a hard shove. Gravity, that bitch, takes care of the first part of his directions. The cheap flip-flops skid a foot after hitting a large patch of wet leaves. My arms are whirling to stay upright as my feet sail into the air. I grunt in pain, my ass smacking to the asphalt.

Wetness soaks my backside as I blink up at the starless night sky.

The crack of skin against skin slices through the silence. Shouts from unfamiliar voices, too close. Pitching forward, I slap my hands on the pathway. On all fours, I crawl to the edge of the sidewalk to a spot dipped in shadows. I blink to reset my contacts, clearing my vision.

The scene in front of me still doesn't make sense.

One man stands above two others writhing on the ground at his feet. The man scans the area, searching. Honey brown eyes pause, locking with mine. Hair a mess, jacket ruffled, he gives a cocky smirk. I release my held breath with a whoosh.

With one more kick to each man's ribs, Trey marches toward me, his strides fast and sure.

"We need to move. Now." Hands tucked under my shoulders, he hauls me upright. "They won't stay down for long. Didn't want to add manslaughter to tonight's events."

I suck in a quick breath with a frantic nod. Right. Good plan.

We race down the path, my flip-flops sliding on the pavement. His grip on my elbow tightens to keep me from falling. After a few minutes of our fast pace, a stitch stabs at my side and my lungs burn. I wheeze, tugging against his hold to tell him to slow down, but he jerks us off the path. I slide along wet grass as I trail behind him, trying to keep up as he pulls us farther along.

A large bolder juts out of the ground up ahead, catching my eye. With a sharp tug, I divert us toward the rock, desperate for a break. The uneven surface pokes at my ass and back when I slump onto it in exhaustion.

I track Trey as he paces back and forth just in front of where I collapsed, never going more than one foot in either direction.

"That was intense," I say between breaths. Maybe I should move cardio up on the to-do list when we get back. "You pushed me."

Trey pauses, tipping his head back. "That's what you want to focus on right now?"

"Yeah. You should apologize." I'm kidding, but the tension radiating off him is freaking me out. I need something to distract him or he'll wear a rut into the soft earth beneath his pounding feet. "I fell on my ass. It hurts."

He slides his hands into the pockets of his slacks and steps forward to stand directly in front of me. Pushing up, I rest both elbows back and cock my head.

"I saved your life, and you want me to apologize for getting you out of the way?"

I nod. A new, sizzling tension pulses between us. The chill in the air evaporates. My skin heats, my pulse skyrocketing higher and tighter.

I hold a tight breath as he leans closer. His large hands rest against the rock on either side of my hips. Shifting closer, he pauses, our faces an inch apart.

"I'm not sorry." His warm breath brushes against my cheek, and my eyes flutter closed on a sigh. "Randi." My name is a desperate plea on his lips. I peel my eyes open, locking onto his. "What are you doing to me?"

"I don't know," I breathe. "But we shouldn't." I reach up, my damp, trembling fingers hovering just over his cheek. "But I can't stop either."

"It's dangerous." He tilts his head, pressing his hot cheek into my awaiting palm. Rough facial hair from his five-o'clock shadow prickles my fingertips as I brush them across his face. His brown eyes shutter closed. "This can't happen."

I ghost my fingers over his temple, across his forehead. Soft, silky dark strands of his hair glide past my hand as I rake it over his scalp down to the base of his neck.

"Fuck," he says on a forced breath. "You're killing me, Randi. Stop."

"I told you," I whisper. Sitting up a fraction, I shorten the distance between our lips. "I can't. I want this." A zap of blazing heat scorches through my core at the brush of my lips against his. "No, Trey, I *need* this."

A truer statement has never been said. I need him. Right here, right now.

His answering growl sends another bolt of excitement and want to the apex of my thighs.

"Anyone could walk up." I whimper at the thought. His answering chuckle is dark and seductive. I suck in a sharp inhale at his soft lips pressing against the sensitive skin of my neck. "You like that, don't you? Didn't expect that."

I give his hair a sharp tug in response to his tentative nip just below my ear.

"Trey," I beg.

He rips the hat off my head, fingers delving into my hair and gripping a section at the base. I gasp at the dominance in his hold. Soft lips brush against my own, teasing. I can't move; desperation ratchets higher and higher.

"This never happened," he growls, then seals his lips over mine. I groan into his mouth, pushing in a plea for more. His hand dips beneath my loose sweatshirt, his callused palm scraping along my stomach.

Pushing off the rock, I arch into his touch. Higher and higher his hand slides. Deft fingers dip inside my bra, yanking the cup low so my breast spills over.

My thoughts whirl. Normally this is when I'm ready for the guy to stick it in and get the show on the road. But now, here with Trey... I'm actually longing for each touch. Every kiss and swipe of his tongue along mine makes the throb between my thighs pulse with more need.

His lips curl against mine in a smile as he pinches my pebbled nipple between his thick fingers. I cry into his mouth as pain and pleasure mix. Panting, I tip my head back and shove my breast into his hand, begging for more.

Fuck, that was hot.

Another tight pinch, this time with a quick twist. I cry out, only for it to be smothered by his palm sealing to my lips. "Good girl," he praises.

I whimper into his palm at the loss of the hand from my breast. Not wasting any time, he dips a hand below the waistband of my sweatpants, sliding over the front of my satin thong.

"Yes," I mumble. The hand at my mouth disappears, replaced by his demanding mouth once again. I nip at his lower lip like I've fantasized.

With the heel of his hand, he presses against my clit, rotating in slow circles.

More. I need more.

The uneven rock snags the cotton sweatpants as I spread my legs wide, giving him access to do his worst.

Two fingers dip beneath my panties, sliding easily through the building slickness.

"Holy fuck." He rips his lips from mine before pressing them to my neck. "If we were somewhere safe…. I want to see all of you. See this soaked pussy, lick up every last drop."

Yes, please.

My elbow slips. Carefully he guides me back, releasing the hold on my hair and resting me against the cold stone.

Low gray clouds blow through the sky above me before my eyes shutter closed. I arch against the boulder as two thick fingers tease outside my slick entrance, plunging in an inch before slowly easing out.

"You're the most fascinating woman I've ever met, Randi Sawyer. And you smell—" He dips low, pressing his nose between my thighs and giving an exaggerated sniff, "—fucking delicious."

Accenting his dirty words, both fingers plunge deep.

I bite down on my forearm to keep from screaming out.

Reaching down, I grip his wrist as it jerks in pounding strokes. I rock forward, meeting the relentless push of his fingers.

Higher and higher I float above the world, every nerve, sensation, and thought focused on the ball of energy building deep in my core. Sweat drips along my hairline. Goose bumps spread over my stomach at exposure to the chilly night air.

I whimper, shaking my head against the rock.

"Come on, Mess. Give it up," Trey commands. The deep rumble of his demanding voice combined with a pinch and twist at my pebbled nipple sets off an explosion.

I sink my teeth into my arm, but still my scream of pleasure echoes around us. My thighs squeeze together, capturing his hand, but his fingers continue to pound deep, prolonging the mind-altering orgasm.

"Holy fuck," I pant, reality settling back in as I come down from my high.

Tipping my chin, I look down my body to where Trey's hand still rests inside my pants. I glance up to his face. His hooded eyes are focused on where his hand cups my mound.

"Trey?" I whisper.

"We need to go," he responds, eyes sliding up to meet mine.

I bite back a whimper as he withdraws his fingers, leaving me achingly empty. Embarrassment warms my cheeks, my movements jerky as I fix my bra and underwear. Trey backs up a step as I push off the rock to stand. I keep my eyes to the ground, attempting to conceal the self-conscious thoughts sprinting through my mind.

"Stop." I jerk my head up, brows raised. "Don't do that. Don't think anything negative. We have to leave because I can't focus on anything other than you, and that's dangerous for both of us. Anyone could've walked up just now and I wouldn't have detected them, too wrapped up in the feel of your pussy squeezing the fuck out of my fingers and imagining my…." My eyes dip to where he grips his crotch and adjusts himself. "Fuck. We need to go, or I'll fucking toss caution to the wind and take you right here."

"I'm okay with that," I say, a shy smile tugging at my lips.

"I'm not going to fuck you in the middle of the park on a damn rock. You deserve better than that, Randi." Debatable. "Plus, we need to get back before Tank calls in the national guard looking for us.

We're already going to pay for being out this late. Don't want to push our luck too much in one night."

Leaning forward, he presses his lips against my forehead. I let my eyes flutter closed as a deep, relaxed exhale eases my racing mind. We both know this can't happen again, that *we* can't happen.

But knowing it can't happen doesn't mean it won't.

CHAPTER EIGHTEEN

RANDI

OCTOBER

S tuck with a dangerously hot man nearly around the clock is torture in itself. Add in the unforgettable memory of his hand between my thighs, the erotic pain shooting from my nipples dampening my center, and I'm a woman on the edge of sanity. For the third time in as many seconds, my attention flicks from the iPad in my hands to where Trey lies sprawled along the couch, eyes closed. His chest rises and falls with each deep, relaxed breath.

How is he not wound up too? Does he not feel the thick sexual tension that's only worsened these past few weeks? The easy smiles he's given me since that night, the sexy smirks and casual laughter, make me wonder if it's just me feeling it.

Surely not.

Surely.

Right?

"What, Mess?" Trey peeks an eye open. "Stop chewing your nails."

I drop the finger from my nibbling teeth. "Okay, Dad."

He closes his eye once again and smirks. Oh, how I want to smack —or kiss—that smirk right off his face.

Ugh, this man is driving me crazier then I already am.

I purse my lips and turn my focus back to the iPad. I've already memorized the possible questions for the debate tonight, but with a few hours to kill before I have to get ready, I might as well review them again. Being overly prepared is how I graduated with honors in undergrad and law school. For those seven years, I averaged three hours a sleep a night, but I did what I had to do. Unfortunately, that sleep cycle stayed with me after I graduated and moved back home. Nowadays, I get around four to five hours a night, but with the stress of the upcoming election, I've reverted back to the measly three.

I groan as the screen blurs once again and toss the iPad to the vacant chair beside me. Letting my head fall against the back of my chair, I close my eyes and press the heels of both hands against my lids.

"I'm so ready for this to be done," I mutter.

"Tonight's the last debate before the election, right?"

Eyes still squeezed shut, I nod. "Thank fuck. I enjoy a good debate, don't get me wrong, but I'm so tired of monitoring the polls, constantly being on edge."

"It won't stop if you win."

I roll my head along the soft cushion and open my eyes, smiling up at T.

"Yes and no. It will be exhausting in a different way. I'm just tired of this posturing, the constant need to be invited to sit at the cool kids' lunch table."

Trey laughs from his spot on the couch.

"We need to leave in four hours," T says, looking at his watch. "I'm meeting with the vice president's alpha team lead downstairs in five to go over the security plans for tonight." He shoots a glare at Trey before turning to me. "Can you two stay out of trouble while I'm gone?"

"Come on, big guy," Trey says, swinging his legs over the side of the couch to sit up. "It's been weeks since 'the incident.' We've been good ever since." I smile at the smirk and wink Trey tosses my way.

"You go handle whatever you need. I promise we won't leave the condo." Three fingers in the air, he adds, "Scout's honor."

"You were never a Boy Scout," T grunts in an almost laugh. He runs a hand up and over his shiny bald head. "I don't have a choice, since the other guys are downstairs securing the building. I'll be back in an hour, two tops." At the door, he turns with a resigned look.

"For fuck's sake," Trey grumbles. "We'll be fine. You act like she died in New York."

I seal my lips together to hide my growing smile. We chose to keep the muggers and what happened after out of the story we gave T when we made it back to the jet that night. No need for him to worry when nothing bad happened.

"Keep him in line," T says, eyes on me.

I hold up three fingers. "Scout's honor."

He grumbles something about us being ridiculous and an accident waiting to happen. I'm still giggling when the door clicks shut behind him and the snap of the deadbolt sounds. Smiling, I turn to Trey, but my smile falters at what I find. I swallow past the stalled breath caught in my throat.

His eyes sparkle with restrained lust. Arms stretched out wide along the back of the couch, he widens his legs and arches a brow. "Two hours alone. What trouble can we get into all alone, Mess?"

My heart thunders against my chest. Holy hell, is this the first time we've been alone since New York?

Untucking my knees from where I'm curled in the chair, I stand on shaking legs. Toes pressed into the thick carpet, I tiptoe to the couch, pausing between his legs. A breath catches in my chest, my eyes closing as his wide hands grip my waist.

"Every day I've watched you knowing what you feel like, smell like. Fucking torture." He sits straight, pressing his face between my thighs into my thin cotton yoga pants. "I shouldn't be this wrapped up in you, Mess. But I can't stop wanting you." He tilts his face up, locking on my eyes. I stroke a hand through his hair, savoring the way it slides between my fingers.

"Then don't," I nearly plead. "I don't want you to hold back."

There's so much I want to tell him. How his touch means so much more than any others. How I don't want to pull away but grow more desperate with each passing minute, each day he doesn't hold me close.

Gripping the hem of my long-sleeve T-shirt, he slides it up, exposing my stomach. Both hands slide into his hair, gripping chunks at the press of his wet lips just below my belly button. I suck in a breath and hold it as the tip of his tongue traces the skin just above my pants. Hooking his thumbs into the waistband, he tugs them an inch lower, repeating the same path with his tongue. Lower and lower my pants drop. My pulse races through my veins, and heat builds beneath my skin.

"I'll never get enough of your scent." His lips move against the sensitive skin above my mound. "It's even hotter knowing how wet I'll find you." Light brown eyes flick up, meeting mine. "And I've barely touched you. Tell me, Mess. Do you want me to lick it up?"

Oh fuck, that's dirty.

And oh, oh so hot.

"Yes," I whisper.

Eyes still locked with mine, he nips at my skin, grinning. "Say it."

"I... I...," I stammer. "I want you to... want you to lick it up. Fuck, please."

"Good—" His next word snaps off. I stumble back as he bolts from the couch. I blink, eyes wide, staring at the gun now in his hand. "Get behind me." I hastily duck behind him, my back to the wall, and tug my pants up. "Grab hold of my jacket and don't let go, you hear me?"

"What's going on?"

"Someone is at the door," he says over his shoulder as we move across the room. "They tried to get in, but the key didn't work."

I gasp. If T hadn't suggested I change my locks last week for increased security measures....

I shriek and jump backward, tugging Trey with me, at a pounding on the door.

Trey shoots an unamused glance over his shoulder and down to me.

"What? I didn't go to spy school. I'm nervous."

His brows tug together. "You do know the difference between the Secret Service and the CIA, right? You might not get my vote if you don't."

I give his jacket a sharp tug and glance to the door that's now shaking from the constant banging on the other side. "You're going to vote for me?"

He shrugs and turns to face the door, but I catch a hint of a smirk on his lips before he does. "Maybe. Now let's see who's knocking, shall we?"

Gun aimed at the door, Trey inches closer and rests his free hand on the deadbolt.

The fabric of his jacket bunches under my tightening fists.

With a quick flip of the lock and a tug on the doorknob, he swings around, blocking the opening with his body.

"What the hell are you doing here?" Trey bites out. His back muscles tense beneath my fists.

Still unable to see, I push to my tiptoes and peer over his shoulder.

"Seriously?" The building anticipation drains from my taut muscles, leaving them heavy and lethargic. Grumbling under my breath, I turn on my bare heels, shuffle back to the center of my condo's living room, and fall into a chair. "What do you want, Shawn?"

"Out of my way, rent-a-cop." Shawn shoulders past the fuming Trey and steps into the living room. In slow motion, Trey turns from the door, shoulders tense, his furious gaze following Shawn's every move.

"Watch it, Shawn," I bite out. It's one thing for them to make fun of me, but my friends? Hell no. "That man can smoosh that narcissistic, smug-ass look right off your ugly face. Not a smart move to piss him off."

Shawn's eyebrows rise a fraction, but the Botox in his forehead prevents them from climbing higher. "Is that so, Trailer?" The shock morphs into his signature smug sneer. "Been getting close to the help, have we?" Delicate fingers pop the button of his suit jacket as he folds onto the couch. "I'd say that's beneath you, but we both know there's not much in this world that is."

Trey's features darken as he takes a menacing step toward the asshole sitting on my couch. I hold up a hand, stopping his advancement.

"As lovely as this all is, what the fuck do you want, Shawn?"

He chuckles, smoothing out the front of his pristine blue dress shirt. "Make sure you're all set for tonight." His ice-blue eyes flick up to mine. "I am your trusted advisor, after all."

"Forced advisor, never trusted," I point out. "And yes, I'm ready. I was reviewing the potential questions one last time when you tried to get in." I narrow my eyes. "When did you get a key?"

"When did you change your locks?"

"Motherfucker," Trey hisses. "How the fuck did you get a key?"

Shawn simply smiles his Joker-like smile. "I have my sources." His attention shifts from Trey back to me. "Tell me, Trailer, is there something going on between you and the wash-up behind me?"

"Not that it matters, but no." Keeping my eyes on Shawn instead of flicking to Trey takes every last drop of resistance I have in my body. "Nothing is going on between us."

"I don't believe you."

Fuck. Not that I would care if people knew Trey and I are fooling around, but not Shawn. He'll find some way to use it against me, use it against Trey. I lose the internal fight and give Trey a pleading look. He doesn't notice, his attention solely on a patch of wall slightly above my head.

I swallow past the rising panic.

"It would be a shame, wouldn't it?" Shawn says, cutting through the uncomfortable silence. "For Benson to lose the job he so loves for a chance at a cunt that's already been passed around most of DC under Kyle's bidding." His eyes flash in victory. He doesn't know Trey knows the truth, everything. Even still, unease rolls my gut. What if Trey believes him? "Not to mention the media circus that would ensue at yet another disastrous relationship for him." He clicks his tongue. "His family name dragged through the media mud once again."

What?

When confusion furrows my dark brows, power lights in those evil eyes. "Ah, I see he hasn't told you everything. Well, it's a good thing I can fill you in—"

"Out," Trey bellows, stalking toward Shawn. Panic replaces the earlier victory in the asshole's wide eyes. "Get out now."

Not waiting for a reply, Trey wraps a hand around the back of Shawn's neck, hauling him off the couch.

"Get your hands off me," Shawn yells. "You'll regret this, Benson. I'll ruin you, ruin your family."

Trey's pounding feet don't falter as he flings the door open, slamming it against the wall. The crack of plaster sounds through the condo. With a final shove from Trey, Shawn stumbles out into the hallway. His face is beet red, nostrils flaring when he turns furious eyes on Trey.

"This isn't over." I blanch, shifting back in the chair when his focus turns on me. "You will pay for this, both of you."

The entire condo shakes at the slam of the door. I flinch at the sound.

Trey's shoulders rise and fall in quick succession, his palms sealed to the closed door, head hanging.

What the hell just happened?

I snap my attention back to Trey from where it'd fallen to the floor. Phone at his ear, he mumbles something, pauses with a silent nod, and then slides the phone from his face. He still hasn't turned.

Confusion morphs into hurt tinged with anger.

"What the hell was all that about?" My voice shakes with the swirl of emotions I can't get a handle on. "I know you said you two had a history, but what he said about another disastrous relationship? Media circus? What the hell, Trey?"

Time stands still. He releases a loud, resigned sigh.

"Look at me," I demand. I swallow back the unshed tears clogging my throat.

"Grem will be here shortly. Don't leave."

"Trey?" I can't keep the pain from seeping into my tone.

Why does my heart ache? He owes me nothing. I shouldn't care. But I do. Fuck, I do. Each heavy thud of my heart sends another aching pang through my chest.

"Good luck tonight," he mumbles in goodbye.

Anger at myself and rejection from his avoidance mix, needing an outlet. I furiously scan the room. Snatching the iPad from the other chair, I hurl it across the room with a banshee scream. The screen splinters against the wall before the device falls to the carpet with a deafening thump.

Chest heaving, I focus on the destroyed electronic.

At least now I'm not the only broken thing in this fucking room.

CHAPTER NINETEEN

TREY

"**W**hat are you doing here?"

Ignoring the beta team member's question, I turn to close and lock the door. I wince at the dented, crumbling section of wall behind it. I need to remember to have that fixed. It was my fault, after all. Normally I keep a tight leash on my anger, keeping it from boiling over—unlike earlier. But Shawn fucking Whit shoved me headfirst over the threshold of my normal hold on that dangerous emotion.

What he said wasn't so much the issue; the disrespect toward Randi was what pushed me past my normal control. She might not have caught it, but I sure fucking did.

I give my head a small shake. Today was a disaster, which morphed into an even bigger disaster at the debate. It couldn't have gone worse for Randi. There's little doubt that the way I left things messed with her concentration.

I'm an idiot. An asshole and an idiot.

If she loses because of me….

"I need to talk to her," I say, turning back toward the living room. One guy sits on the couch, the rest of the team outside in the hall or downstairs at all the entry points.

"Not sure that's a good idea," the guy says with a laugh. "Birmingham just left. I heard every word. He ripped her a new one. If I were her, I'd be in there packing my bags with my damn tail between my legs."

I don't suppress my deep groan.

This apology will be expensive. Even something from Tiffany's might not make up for the last twelve hours.

Earlier, I retreated, not ready to admit why Shawn's words and insults to Randi hit deep. I needed a few hours to process it alone. Could I have told her all that so she didn't have to wonder all day? Yeah, but at the time, the rage clouded my vision; all I could see was my own pain.

"Tank asked me to come up and talk about tomorrow." Lie. "We need to go over a few things, so I might be a while." Truth. "Take a break. I've got this for a few hours."

He shrugs and lies back on the couch. "Don't have to tell me twice. Thanks, Benson."

Hand on the doorknob to the bedroom, I pause. Nervous energy builds, my chest tightening.

She has to forgive me.

I don't knock. With a quick twist of the knob and a push of the door, I step into her bedroom. Grief permeates the air, smacking me in the face. Each breath deepens the regret filling my chest.

"Randi." Not taking my eyes off where she's perched on the edge of the bed, I reach back, closing the door and flicking the lock. She doesn't acknowledge me, her eyes glued to the opposite wall. "Mess." Each step is tentative, careful, like I'm approaching a wounded animal. Technically I guess I am. Her, the most fascinating woman I've ever met, me, the one who hurt the insecure person she hides beneath the Political Barbie mask.

"What do you want, Benson?"

I cringe. Benson, not Trouble. Hell, not even Trey. Not a good sign.

Determination propels me forward, sitting me beside her. The bed dips, rocking her an inch closer.

"I wanted to check in on you." She huffs, her eyes rolling to the ceiling. "To apologize."

"Little late for that, don't you think?" She shoves her hands on the bed, pushing herself up. Slowly she turns to face me, meeting my pleading gaze for the first time since I entered the room. "You saw the debate?" Her shoulders slump. "I lost us the election tonight." Her eyes, brightened to a perfect green by the stupid contacts Kyle makes her wear, look to the ceiling. "I'm ruined. I'll have to go back home, failing again." Her gaze is still upturned as a single tear trickles down her cheek.

Pain like I've never experienced cuts through my chest, piercing my heart.

"It's too late. You left when all I needed was an explanation. You left me, confused, angry…." Her throat bobs. "Hurt. Fucking hell, Trey. You hurt me by not caring enough to stay and tell me what the hell all that between you and Shawn was. I didn't care—I don't care—what he says. I know every word out of his mouth has an agenda, some form of power play." Pain, anger, and, the worst, disappointment cloud her beautiful face when she finally looks back down. "You don't owe me anything. This, what we did in the park, the flirting back and forth, you don't owe me anything, but what hurt was that you didn't even stop to think I deserved an explanation. You just walked out, making me feel…." She stomps her foot against the carpet. "You made me feel as worthless as everyone else has my entire life."

I don't think, only react to the ripping, shredding of my heart.

Reaching out, I yank her into my arms, holding her close, squeezing her tight.

"I'm sorry," I plead into her hair. "Fuck, I'm sorry." Her shoulders shake. I tighten my hold. "Tell me what to do. Tell me what to say, what to buy. I'm so sorry, Mess. I fucked up. I couldn't… I didn't know how to…. It was me. All me. I was so angry at Shawn, I couldn't think past the need to beat the shit out of him."

Her soft dark hair slides beneath my palm as I stroke it over and over. With each breath, I apologize all over again. Time slows; nothing outside of the woman in my arms matters. Eventually her breaths even out, the shoulder-racking sobs ceasing.

So much needs to be said, needs to be explained, but the moment is still too raw for more words.

Her body molds into mine, folding between my arms as I lift her and walk across the room. Inside the bathroom, I carefully set her on the white marble counter, holding her shoulders to make sure she's steady before stepping toward the tub. Fingers beneath the heavy stream of water, I wait until it turns scorching hot and close the drain. Searching through the various bottles along the edge, I pluck a bottle of cherry vanilla bubble bath and dump a drop into the water. I frown at the small amount of bubbles that break the surface. Twisting off the cap, I tip the bottle over, emptying the entire contents into the water.

It takes a whole bottle per bath, right?

Fuck if I know.

I toss the empty bottle into the trash can across the room; it clatters against the metal sides as it descends to the bottom. I lift both hands into the air, pumping my fists in victory. Wearing a tentative smile, I chance a look to Mess. My heart leaps at the small smile she's desperately trying to not let me see.

"I'm going back to a life of destitution, and you're cheering over making an easy toss."

I look from her to the trash can and back again. "Easy? Like to see you do it." Her smile grows, bunching her adorable cheeks. "You're not going back. The election isn't over. We can figure it out, but first...." I point to the half-filled bathtub and overflowing bubbles. "Shit, maybe I put too much in."

"You think?" she says with a huffed laugh.

"Take a bath, relax. Then we'll talk." I pause at the door and look over my shoulder. "If you need anything, let me know. I'll be right outside the door."

At her nod, I step into the bedroom, closing the door behind me. The hinges give a tight rattle at the weight of my back slamming against the cool wood.

Now to come up with a plan to keep her in DC. If today taught me anything, it's that I'm not ready for her to be out of my life. Not yet. Hell, maybe not ever.

———————

"You look better," I say with a smile as she steps out of the bathroom. "How do you feel?"

"Better." The tension around her eyes still creases the edges, but the weight from earlier seems lifted for the moment. "Thanks for that." Her fingers fidget with the sash of her terry cloth robe. "Now what?" Her hopeful gaze meets mine.

Pinkie nail between her teeth, she shuffles across the room and plops down onto the bed, staring at me.

"First"—I turn, bringing a bent leg to the bed to face her straight on—"I need to explain today, what happened with Shawn." I clear my throat and grip the pant leg of my old jeans to keep from reaching for her. "I didn't know what to think when you stood up for me. Called him out for me."

A single shoulder rises and falls in a noncommittal shrug. The movement widens the gap of her robe a fraction, exposing more of the soft skin concealed beneath. "No one makes fun of my friends and gets away with it. I'm a bit protective, I guess."

I smirk. "Ditto, Mess. Which is why today blew the roof off the normal restraint I have on my anger. Hearing him call you... well, you were there. You know what he said." I tighten my right hand into a fist. "And I couldn't do a damn thing. I knew if I did, it would come back and hurt you. Hell, me being in the room already did some of that. He wouldn't have pressed you, pushed you, if I wasn't there. If I wasn't in the picture at all."

I huff out a deep breath and look to the ceiling.

"It's always been like this. Between Shawn, Kyle, and me, we've always been at each other's throats, vying for the upper hand. So what you saw today was all about me and Shawn, about our shit, not you, but I pulled you into it. That pissed me off."

"Not trying to be a dick here," she says with a shove to my shoulder, "but that's really arrogant of you."

I whip my gaze to where she leans back against the headboard. "What?"

"Shawn already hated me. He might have found a new angle to push my buttons, but nothing about today started with you. It started the minute he caught me sniffing the wallpaper last year."

"Um, what?" I chuckle. *This woman.*

She swipes her hand through the air in dismissal. "All I'm saying is you're taking responsibility for something that isn't yours to take. I knew stepping into this spot, have known since I met Shawn, that he'll use anything and everything he can to bring me down." Her gaze turns unfocused. "Do you think he'd say something to the media about us? Try to sabotage the campaign even though Kyle's his friend?"

An incredulous chuckle rumbles in my chest. "One hundred percent hell yes. I think he already did."

Her mouth pops in shock, opening wide.

I can't help the dirty track my mind takes me down at the sight. I swipe my tongue along my lower lip. Oh, the things I want to do to those plump lips.

"You think he came over today with the intention of derailing my focus."

I nod.

"That motherfucking cuntcake."

"Always has been."

Her head thumps against the headboard, her eyes squeezing shut. "Well, he got what he wanted. Tonight was horrible."

"Well," I say as I lie back on the bed, tucking both hands beneath my head, "it wasn't great. But it doesn't mean it's all for not. On the way over here, the various anchors were saying it was a tie. You did good. Not great, but you didn't bomb it like you're thinking you did."

"That's not what Kyle thinks." She sighs.

"He's a fucking drama queen, has been his whole life. It's not as bad as you think." I cut my eyes to meet hers. "But nothing else can happen to derail your focus or shift the attention off your campaign points. You need to get back out there, hit the swing states hard. Remind them that you do know your shit, and you're the one who will have their backs. Remind them of your original platform. You're their voice in DC."

"Why aren't you my advisor?" she asks, arching both brows in question. "You seem to know a lot about all this."

"I was raised in this life. My parents wanted me to take a political path, but I didn't. Once I stepped away from it, I saw it for what it was, and I wanted no part of playing the political game the rest of my life. That's when I went into the army. It saved me from being a conniving, miserable fuckstick like everyone else in this town."

"What did Shawn mean by a media circus, a disastrous relationship?" Gripping the edges of her robe tighter, she slides down the bed, lying at my side, head propped up with an elbow digging into the mattress.

"Ah, that." I roll to face her, mirroring her pose. "The girl I was dating last year was the purest definition of a power-hungry political pawn."

"Ah, the person you thought I was at first." My gaze traces the curve of her lips as they move up her face in a sassy smile. "This mystery woman is the one I can thank for the incorrect judgments you spouted my way."

"Yep. Something happened, I did something last year that caused our team to be demoted. It was a rough patch, and during that time, she showed her true self. Later on, I learned my parents were in her ear, trying to get her to convince me to step back into the political scene. I was the idiot who went over a year not realizing she was playing me." Reaching out, I fiddle with the sash of her robe that lays in the small distance between us. "My family is one of the bigger names in politics. More behind the scenes, but they're the money to a lot that goes on in this city. That's what Rachel wanted. The power that comes with my name, the trust fund. Not me," I grumble and roll my eyes.

"So she left you because...."

"For Shawn fucking Whit." Randi's eyes widen to a comical size. "Yep. Apparently even my family name and millions in the bank couldn't cover the embarrassment she felt for being with a demoted Secret Service agent."

"I hate her." An evil smirk forms. "Wait. If she's with Shawn... oh, this will be fun."

Apprehension pulls me back an inch, scanning her face. "What?"

"Don't worry, Trouble."

"That's not reassuring." I give the terry cloth belt a hard tug. "What are you planning?"

Randi shrugs and flops back to the bed.

"Oh no you don't." The bed dips beneath my weight, and a shriek of surprise squeaks past her smiling lips. Hovering over her, I pull my face close, our noses a hairbreadth apart.

Her smile falls, her eyes slipping to focus on my lips. Her heaving chest presses her breasts tighter against me. A moan pushes past my lips, brushing across her face and fogging the lenses of her glasses. Pinching the frames between two fingers, I tug them free and toss them across the bed.

I rake the tips of my fingers through her dark hair, causing her eyes to shutter closed.

Each inch between us is the kind of torture that drives men insane. Her lips pucker, demanding more at the faint brush of my own. The softness of her lips ease the growing ache that's been building since Shawn interrupted us. I groan into her mouth at the shift of her hips, the spread of her legs beneath me.

"Randi," I whisper against her lips, then seal mine over hers, needing more. Tugging on her hair, I angle her head to deepen the kiss, taking control of the pace.

Her hands slide between us, gripping the hem of my black T-shirt. I lift up, helping her yank it over my head. Goose bumps spread across my back at her delicate strokes up and down my skin. I move my body against hers, eliciting a moan of pleasure from both our lips.

Sucking on her neck, I then nip beneath her ear. With a flex of my hips, I press my steel-hard cock against her core.

"Oh fuck," she whispers, squeezing her eyes shut.

The sweet scent of her arousal meets my nose, driving me lower.

Gripping the inside edges of her robe, I slowly spread it apart, exposing the bare skin of her chest inch by inch. Her full breasts bounce with each of her sharp inhales. Eyes locked with hers, I lower my lips to a pebbled nipple, flicking the tip of my tongue against it before taking a quick, hard nip. Back arching off the bed, Randi threads her fingers through my hair, pushing her breast into my waiting mouth.

Her body writhes beneath me, each wiggle causing her to press against my cock.

The touch of her fingers at my waistband makes me pull back, dipping my chin to watch. The first few times, the button fails to pop at her demanding fingers, but eventually it gives, and the grind of the zipper lowering catches my breath. Her hand dips in, wrapping around my dick. I thrust into her palm, devouring the sensation of another's touch when I've gone so long without.

Knee to the bed, I press off and stand. Taking in every inch of her near-naked body sprawled across the bed, waiting for me, I toe off my tennis shoes and let my jeans puddle to the floor. I hiss in a breath, wrapping a hand around myself and squeezing tight.

"Condom?" she pants.

I nod and retrieve my wallet from my jeans, tugging the condom out and tossing the wallet to the floor. I rip the wrapper up and roll the thin rubber down my hard length.

"Is this what you want?" I ask, giving my cock another hard squeeze. Fuck, this isn't going to last long. It's been way too long, and the building fire between us is on the verge of an all-engulfing inferno.

A flush spreads across her fair cheeks, highlighting her freckles. Biting her lip, she responds with a shaky nod.

I start at her ankles, softly stroking the tips of my fingers up and down her skin, rising higher with each pass. The edges of the robe fall away, pooling at her side.

"This is dangerous," I mutter to myself. "This changes everything."

There's no coming back from this, from her.

Ask me if I fucking care.

CHAPTER TWENTY

RANDI

I can't breathe. No air will fill my lungs, even though I'm sucking in as much as I can with each short breath.

Holy hotness, the man is like the Italian statues I've seen in textbooks. He's strong but not bulky, lean and toned. Muscles bunch with every move he makes, snapping taut beneath his soft tan skin. A smatter of chest hair covers the space between his pecs, disappearing down his rippled stomach until reappearing just below his navel.

My gaze follows the well-named happy trail, pausing on his thick cock, mesmerized by each tug of his hand up and down his shaft. I lick my lips, desperate to lean forward for a taste. Up and down his hand moves, that damn smirk causing even more dampness to gather between my thighs.

So this is what handsy sex should've been like my whole life.

Or maybe handsy sex is only good with Trouble.

Hmm, need to think that through. Later.

His hands brush up my legs, shoving away the offending scraps of robe that still cover parts of my body. Over my waist, up my chest, lingering to pinch and twist both aching nipples, his hands finally dip beneath my shoulders, tugging the robe lower down my back.

"What the—" His mouth hangs open, eyes wide, focused on my right shoulder. I give it a little wiggle. "You have a tattoo. Tattoos."

I nod, reaching up and running my fingers across his chest. Touching him is a compulsion; I couldn't stop myself even if I drained every last drop of energy into trying.

He yanks the sleeve of the robe lower. "How far does it go?"

"My elbow." Reaching down, I wrap my hand around him. "Can we talk about this later?"

Hooded eyes meet mine as I stretch between us, squeezing him tight. Trouble's lids slam shut as his hips drive forward. The head skims between my folds, grazing my clit.

"Trey," I whine. I should be embarrassed, but I'm not—at all. This is fucking fantastic and terrible and wonderful all at the same time. The anticipation of what's to come, the feel of him inside me, is almost too much to contain.

He dips forward, his teeth latching onto a peeked nipple while his tongue flicks furiously, barely connecting and driving me crazy. I slide the rubber-covered tip up and down my slit, teasing myself while arching my chest against his torturous mouth.

He grips my wrist, tugging my hand away. My whimper morphs into a relieved moan as he pushes the first inch of his hard length inside me. He moves in slow, calculated strokes, pulling all the way out before plunging deeper than before.

Sweat beads along his forehead, gathering to drip down his temples.

I moan, but he quickly presses his lips over mine to quiet the sound. A soft, demanding tongue teases mine, caressing and plunging with expert strokes.

Heat crawls beneath my skin, sweat glistening over every inch and slicking the places where our bodies connect.

Taut energy coils in my gut, sending tremors through my legs. My toes curl, digging into the fluffy, suffocating duvet. Hips rocketing off the bed, I match his thrusts, pushing him deeper. With a lust-filled snarl, he grips both hips, lifting them higher, hitting my elusive G-spot.

"Fuck," I cry out. His palm seals against my lips effectively quieting my curses.

My nostrils flare with each erratic inhale.

"You have to be quiet, baby," Trey says, his voice rough with need. "Can you do that?"

The duvet slips beneath my hair at my urgent nod.

"Good girl." His fingers trace down my chin and along my neck before moving lower. The brush of his thumb against my clit shoots bursts of sparkling sensations to each nerve. My teeth sink into the tip of my tongue, the taste of blood filling my mouth.

Then I shatter, every cell exploding in insistent throbs. Forearm pressed against my parted lips, I scream against my skin. The outside world fades to white noise, my intense pleasure dangling me over an empty chasm where nothing but my orgasm exists.

Trouble grunts a curse, his hips thrusting fast and wild.

I huff a forced exhale at the unexpected weight of him falling above me, pressing my entire body into the mattress.

"I know I'm smothering you," he says into the geometric fabric of the duvet, "but I can't move. Sorry if you die."

My face splits into a wide smile, my cheeks bunching so tight they ache. I stroke up and down his back, slipping lower to brush across his tight ass.

Everything is perfect, calm.

Tomorrow, I'll fight to regain the traction I lost with the failed debate.

Tomorrow, I fight to win.

Because there's no way in hell I can go back now. Not after tonight. Not after him.

Maybe not ever.

———

COULD a moment be any more perfect? I trace the outline of his pouty lower lip, brushing the pad of my finger back and forth. The softness of sleep eases the worry lines of his forehead, relaxing the normal intense focus. His neat brow shifts beneath my stroking.

Sunlight hasn't even begun to peek around the curtains it's so early, but this being the first night he's slept over, I can't find it in me to waste a minute of it sleeping. The past couple weeks of us finding time alone and keeping T's suspicions at bay have been a well-coordinated dance. But even then, moments like this are few and far between.

I trace the shell of his ear, shifting a lock of brown hair to tuck it back.

I've worked my ass off since the disastrous debate. Flying across the country, visiting state after state, trying to raise our poll numbers. And it's working. Our ranking, once steady, now rises with each preliminary poll. Which means we still have a shot to win.

T and Trey are at my side each step of the way, always encouraging and keeping me on point. The whole team has been, really. We've grown close, forming a familial bond since they saved my life two months ago. I'm not ready for that to stop.

I inhale a shaky breath and burrow deeper into the cloud-like pillow.

I'm not ready for any of this to end. It's exhausting, yes, and more work than I expected, but the relationships, the friendships I've built here, I'm not ready to give up. Not yet. It feels like we're all on the verge of something great, something bigger than all of us.

We have to win.

"What are you doing?" Trey mutters into the mattress.

Who sleeps without a pillow?

"Early voting starts today," I whisper into the darkness. Bits of light stream around the blackout curtains. "It's not that early. Look, the sun is starting to come out."

"Tell the sun to hit Snooze. It's my day off." Without opening his eyes, he shifts on the bed, turning his head from my ministrations. "This was not part of the deal of me staying over."

The bed shakes as I silently laugh. There was no deal. Last night, after he pinned me to the wall and had his way with me—three times —I asked him to stay, so he did.

"What time is it, anyway?" His grumbled voice is barely loud enough for me to hear.

I roll to my side and crane my neck back. "Would you believe me if I said close to five?"

The bed shifts as Trey rises up to his elbows, a pointed sleepy-eyed glare directed at me. "That's only four hours of sleep."

I purse my lips to keep from correcting him.

"Randi." His tone is frustrated. "Please tell me you've slept."

"An hour or two," I say with a shrug. "It's normal for me. I can't sleep when I'm stressed."

"You don't eat and you don't sleep." His hair falls across his fore-head with the shake of his head. "Randi, that's not healthy or sustain-able. When you're VP, you have to take better care of yourself." When, not if. I like that. "Tank and I try to help you manage it the best we can, but you have to put in some effort too. We can't make you sleep."

"I know, and I appreciate you and T for all that you do for me. I really do." Flipping to my stomach, I stare at the tufted headboard. "It's just that I've done this life stuff on my own for so long, you know. If we win, I'll get some help, I promise. Maybe a secretary or something; that way all the reminding and babysitting doesn't fall on the team."

"First of all, when you win, not if." I fight the smile trying to spread up my cheeks. "Second, you will need help. You won't be able to do it all on your own like you've done everything else. No one can handle that kind of pressure, understand?"

I roll my head, flopping it to the side to watch him.

"I understand." Reaching up, I trace the underside of his jaw, the morning stubble scraping my finger. "I'll figure it out. I always do." I bite my lip, nervous energy building beneath my skin, flashing heat through my body. "Trey?" I swallow and look over his shoulder, avoiding those knowing brown eyes. "What will happen, with us after the election?" The shake in my voice is proof of the emotions swirling around that single question.

He presses a callused palm to my cheek, swiping his thumb across my cheekbone, sending a shiver racing down my spine. I pull back to meet his gaze.

"I don't know, Randi. I really don't." My eyes fall to the expanse of white sheet between us. "Hey, stop that. Look at me." Scrolling up his bare chest, I meet his eyes once again. "I'm not saying I don't want us to keep doing this, but things will change if you're in the official VP spot. Expectations are higher, the scrutiny more intense—hell, you might not have more than thirty minutes alone until your four years are done. All I'm saying is I don't know what will happen next, but that doesn't take away from this, us, right now, does it?"

Thumbnail between my teeth. I shake my head. "No, no it doesn't. I just... I want to be prepared for what's coming. I feel out of control right now, and I hate it. I need one thing, one sure thing I can hold on to until the election, you know?"

The corners of his lips tug in a knowing smile. "I know, but the reality is anything can happen, and—"

A pounding on the door cuts Trey off, and we both jolt straight up. Trey hops off the bed, yanking his jeans up his thighs before I can blink. He scans the phone in one hand as he attempts to dress with the other.

The jerky movements slow, stopping completely with his T-shirt halfway on. Wide eyes meet mine, his nostrils flaring.

"What?" I breathe. "What happened?"

I ignore the pounding at the door, eyes searching Trey's. His face is paler than moments ago.

"Trey, talk to me." I blindly reach for the nightstand, hand slapping the surface in search of my phone. He races across the room, bare feet pounding against the carpet, snatching it away before I can grab it. "You're freaking me out," I shout.

"Open up," T's demanding, angry, and—if I'm not mistaken—a bit scared voice booms from the other side of the door.

I suck in a breath, eyes flicking to the door. Trey lets out a loud, slow exhale and walks to it, shoving his arms through the sleeves of his T-shirt. The sheets tangle around my legs as I kick them furiously until I'm free, then race to the bathroom. The door isn't all the way closed behind me when the bedroom door slams open.

Each move jerky, I bolt from one side of the bathroom to the other, searching for something to slip on. Once T finds Trouble in my room at this hour, it'll be obvious what he and I were doing, but that doesn't mean I want to confirm his suspicions by popping out there naked. Clothes sail behind me, floating to the tile floor, as I rummage through the dirty laundry.

The black yoga pants have some kind of food stain dotting the left thigh, but the sweatshirt I yank on appears somewhat decent. Whatever, it's just T and Trey. Quick stop for a hair tie and I ease toward the door. The tips of my hair flick and twirl beneath my hands as I wrap it in a makeshift bun.

T's voice vibrates through the painted wood at my face; I don't even have to try and eavesdrop to hear what's being said.

"You've crossed the line this time, Benson."

Oh snap, T is pissed.

"It's not what you think." Trey's tone is tight and low.

"Really? Seems to me you're fucking—"

"Watch it," Trey bites out. "I'm trying to tell you it's not what you think." A pregnant pause has me pressing my ear against the door, not wanting to miss a word. "I like her, okay? It's not just about the sex, but the fact that you think so little of me, that I'd use her like that, fucking hurts."

T mumbles something too low for me to understand.

Screw this.

Taking a big step back, I yank open the door. The two men stand inches apart, their hands curled into tight fists. Neither looks my way.

"Oh stop it, you two. Duke it out later, okay? Right now I need one of you to tell me why I can't check my phone and why T's here so early. What's. Going. On."

T's the first one to break the stare-off, his dark brown eyes finding mine.

"It's out."

"Not following. What's out, T?"

"Your mom. Your life. Plus some sources saying you're cheating on Birmingham with one of your Secret Service agents. It's being covered on every network. Hell, they already have people on location in Boone and camped outside that rehab facility you put your mom in."

I can't breathe. The room spins. All the blood drains from my face, and my hands tremble at my side. Eyes still locked with his, I shake my head, disbelieving his words.

"No, that's… no. It's impossible. Not now."

I stagger back, the wall stopping me from tumbling down. Both men rush across the room, Trey's arms reaching me first. I'm numb, barely registering the tight grip around my waist that keeps me from falling to the floor.

"Easy, Randi," Trey whispers into my hair.

My breaths come in short pants, desperate for small amounts of air.

"Randi, look at me." T's thick fingers wrap around my chin, tipping my gaze up to meet his. "Calm down. You can't solve anything passed the fuck out. Do you hear me?" His voice is stern, commanding. "Get it together. Now."

"Match my breaths, Mess. In." Trey's chest puffs out, pressing against my back. "And out." Wisps of my air float forward on his deep exhale. Over and over he urges me to mirror his deep breaths. After several rounds, the room stills, my vision clearing.

"I'm, okay. I'm… oh fuck." I gasp, clasping a hand around my neck. "This is bad. It's bad, isn't it?"

My eyes frantically search T's for answers.

"It's not good."

"Tell me." I ball my hands into small fists. "Give me my phone."

"Let's get you to sit down first," Trey says, already guiding me across the room. He sits me in the buttercream-colored chair but doesn't go far. Squatting between my legs, he gives a comforting squeeze above both knees.

"How bad is it?" I ask T again.

"The worst are calling you a fraud," he states, zero emotion in his tone, the stone-faced protector mask back in place. I groan, dropping my face into my awaiting palms. "The best are focusing on the cheating angle."

"This couldn't have come at a worse time. Now we have zero time to come up with a new strategy. Early voting starts today."

"The timing is... questionable." I drop my hands, blinking rapidly at T, his tone giving me pause. "I find it odd that right when you're making headway in the polls after that debate, this bomb drops. The timing of everything seems planned. Plotted."

My mouth pops open, gaping wide.

"Holy fuck," I whisper. "You think Shawn did this. You think Shawn's the one who leaked it all." I whip around to face Trey. "Before the debate, he suspected something was going on between us."

T huffs and crosses his trunk-like arms across his broad chest. "Anyone could tell there was something going on between you two if they saw you together." I cringe. "You're an idiot, playboy. I had no idea it was this"—his mitt of a hand waves between us—"deep."

"Whoa. Playboy?" I scoff.

"Can we focus on the issue at hand, please," Trey grumbles, running a hand through his hair. "Why didn't you say anything?" He turns on the balls of his bare feet to face T.

"I thought it was innocent flirting. If I'd known this?" He looks to me and shakes his head. "You both know you're playing with fire, don't you?"

"Is it that bad?" I ask.

"Yes." I shrink back into the chair. "It makes a weak link in the team, puts you at risk, not to mention how it would look to the public. It stops, now." T jabs a finger at Trey. "You know what happened the last time you bent the rules." I turn to Trey. His features are filled with remorse, guilt. "I will not let you sideline this team again. You two end today."

"Not that it matters." Emotions clog my throat. Tears well, stinging my eyes. "Nothing matters. It's over. How can I face the public again? They know I lied."

Trey leans a shoulder against the chair, focusing on the carpet.

"I am a fraud," I whisper, losing all restraint on the tears.

"But you're not," Trey mutters. "Everything is about perception. They only have the side Shawn gave them." He glances up from the floor, eyes locking with my questioning gaze.

"So?"

A smirk tugs at his lips.

Oh no. This could be brilliant or terrifying.

"So, we give them yours. I need something to write on," he says, shoving off the floor and striding away. At the door, he turns, excited energy pulsing off him. "Get dressed in your normal stuff, not the fancy dresses Kyle makes you wear in public. Minimal makeup." His gaze flicks to my unruly hair. "Might want to put a little work into that though. It's a mess, Mess."

"What are you going to do?" I ask, pushing up from the chair.

"Turn the tide."

Only a miracle sprinkled with unicorn blood could turn this clusterfuck around.

Which begs the question: What in the hell is he planning?

CHAPTER TWENTY-ONE

RANDI

I tug down the hem of my green V-neck sweater below the waistband only for it to pop right back up. Glancing out the glass doors to the mob of reporters, I swipe my sweaty palms down the sides of my dark-wash jeans. Like Trey instructed an hour ago, I'm normal Randi. Not the perfect Political Barbie Kyle always demands me to be in public. From the older sweater to my Wranglers and scuffed boots, I'm me. Still fancier then Randi 1.0 but not nearly the obnoxious sparkle of Randi 2.0.

So what does that make this version, Randi 1.5 or Randi 3.0?

Debatable for sure.

"You think this will work?" I ask over my shoulder to where T and Trey huddle with the rest of the team. Several came in on their day off to be here for me. Never in my life have I had this much support. It strengthens my resolve to get this right. My one shot to correct the damage Shawn did by leaking my background to the media. We don't know for certain it was him, of course, but I wouldn't put it past that conniving asshole

"It has to work, Mess."

I turn my attention back to the glass doors.

Due to the size of the University of Texas campus, Taeler is able to lie low until after the press conference, thank goodness. Still, T called in extra security to watch her until the story's initial sensation wears off.

Which it will, hopefully.

"Ready, guys?"

"Ready," the team announces in unison behind me.

I choke back the building tears. Without these men, one in particular, I couldn't get through this shit show.

A blast of bitter wind slashes against my cheeks, blowing my loose hair from one shoulder to the other. I suppress a shudder as I step deeper into the mass of reporters, all yelling my name and demanding answers while cameras snap.

I hold up a hand, hoping it's enough to quiet the crowd.

It's not.

Instead, several in the front lurch forward, propped up by the people behind them, closing the distance between me and them. Trey, T, and the rest of the agents rush forward, shoving the circling vultures back to their original distance.

A full-body tremble bolts down my spine, my hands twitching nervously at my side. This isn't my normal stage, the typical monitored debate. This is real, ugly, and terrifying.

"Everyone calm the hell down," T bellows.

The shouts quiet to murmurs. Seems no one can disobey a direct order from the big guy.

Locking his kind, dark eyes with mine, T nods. An indication for me to get this show on the road.

I clear my throat, widen my stance, and clasp both hands behind my back. Straightening my back, I smile into the crowd.

Here goes... everything.

"I know everyone has questions they want to ask regarding the details of my life which were released early this morning, but I won't be answering them." A chaotic shout of protests answers in response. "What I will do, however, is give you the true story. My story. The truth. All of it. But first I'd like to address the people whom I've misled these past several months." I pause, letting the crowd quiet down. Nostrils flaring, I inhale deeply and continue.

"To my fellow Americans, I'm sorry." I swallow thickly and wet my lips. "I'm not apologizing for the story you were led to believe early on but for being ashamed enough about my past that I felt the need to. I'm here to set the story straight, for you to see the real Randi Sawyer. The good, the bad, and the nitty gritty—and believe me, there's a lot of that. I was born to a teen mother who had no business raising a child but still did. She supported us through welfare and social security fraud and lived in a run-down trailer in the worst trailer park in town, where she went through a new boyfriend every other week.

"I knew early in my childhood that I didn't want her life for my own. I wanted to succeed, to be someone I could be proud of becoming. Most days after school were filled with my closest friends, Blanche, Sophia, Dorothy, and of course the hilarious Rose. There were days when she forgot to buy food, so I learned to depend on myself for everything. Homework, bathing, clothes—everything fell on me from about kindergarten on."

I tighten my hands into fists. Tears threaten as the memories flood through, a heart-shredding tidal wave of knives slamming into my chest.

"I was bullied, made fun of, teased, ignored, all of it. All because of whose daughter I am, of things I couldn't control at such a young age. I tell you this not to make you feel sorry for me or for you to pity my childhood. As neglectful as my mother was, I still had it better than some. I'm telling you this to explain why I did it. My entire life, I've been judged, overlooked, forgotten, and, worst of all, told repeatedly that I'm nothing, a loser, and that I will never, ever break the cycle my mother birthed me into.

"At fifteen, I proved everyone right. I got pregnant by my boyfriend in the back of his parents' van. I thought up to that point the harassment was bad, but oh no, it could get worse. It did get worse. I decided then, after my daughter was born, that I would do everything in my power to make sure my life didn't bleed over into hers. I wanted her to have it all, to be the pretty, popular girl in school that I had never been and would never be.

"Things got a little hairy after she was born. My mom kicked me out to the shed to raise my daughter, the schoolwork was piling on, and I was out of options. CPS was called in, and"—I swipe a lone tear dripping down my cold cheek—"I was devastated. Absolutely devastated. Only weeks old and I was already failing her. The justice system deemed me an unfit mother, giving my child—my daughter who I would've sacrificed my life for—to her biological father's parents. I had to fight to see her, and when I did, the hateful words, shaming, and disgust filled the house from the moment I stepped through the door until I left. It ripped me to shreds.

"Those following weeks changed me. My determination to change my life, to be more than a trailer trash teen mom, strengthened. The parts about me going to UT Austin and then on to Harvard are all true. You can ask any of my professors; I'm certain they haven't forgotten the student who asked for more work every class to stay one step ahead of everyone else."

My gaze floats up to the gray sky.

"How I got to this spot, well, that's another long story, but I'll keep it short. I knew Kyle Birmingham at Harvard, and we hated each other." An uncomfortable chuckle vibrates through the crowd. "After law school I went back to Boone, started my own family law practice to be the voice for the underprivileged, and became mayor to help implement some much-needed changes. One day last year, Kyle walked into my office declaring he wanted to run for office but wanted someone with a 'normal' life to help him see things from the people's perspective." Slight lie, but this is my spin on the truth. "He helped me pay off some of the student loans and other debt that hung around my neck like a boat anchor, got me to DC, and here I am. Here I am pleading for you to understand.

"It had nothing to do with you and everything to do with my fears. I was scared I wouldn't get a chance in this town, a chance to win your vote, if you knew the truth about my background. I've heard too many times the hateful words, the snap judgments people make when they know the truth, and I couldn't risk it.

"So, that's my story. That's the truth. All of it. And I'll tell you one more truth: I want this job. I want to represent you here in Washington. This town is full of people who don't understand the daily struggles of living paycheck to paycheck and the frustration when taxes go up again and less of your hard-earned money comes home. I will be your voice, the slap of reality to this town. If you'll have me."

Two seconds of shocked quiet pulses before the crowd erupts in shouts.

I smile, give a quick wave, and turn to head back into the safety of the lobby.

"What about the cheating rumors?" someone shouts above all the other voices. "A liar and a cheater. Sounds like the same old politician to me."

My steps pause. I suck in a breath and turn back to the cameras.

"Right, forgot about that one. First of all, let's get the thing cleared up about me and Kyle." I have to tread lightly here. The people might forgive me for being ashamed of my past, but admitting to lying about the relationship part might push them over the edge. "What's going on between us is our business. However, I can tell you we've decided we're best as political partners, nothing else. As far as a relationship with a certain agent, that's a load of fiction. I have made a few friends with the men who are at my side day in and day out the past few months. They've had my back and provided me with some great counsel, seeing as this whole political power game is new to me. I had no one to confide in until they arrived. Now I'm happy to say I have friends here—they just to happen to get paid to hang out with me."

I smile at the rumble of laughter.

"Early voting starts today. Go out to the polls, vote. Vote for me, vote for another candidate, but please, please vote. It's your voice, your chance to tell the people in DC who you want representing you. Change can happen, but it won't if you expect others to pull the load. Thank you."

Smiling, I wiggle two fingers in the air like a motherfucking idiot.

Turning on my heels, I speed-walk back to the lobby doors, throwing them open and rushing inside, heat blazing across my face. I press the traitorous fingers to my cheeks, attempting to cool my flush.

"Was that a poor imitation of Nixon?"

I groan and throw my hands into the air in exasperation. "What the hell is wrong with me? I give the best speech of my life and then go do that shit."

"That was pretty bad, Mess." Trey chuckles, his signature smirk pulling at his lips. "Other than that though, I'd say you nailed it. Great job."

Our heavy footsteps echo through the otherwise silent lobby. Trey and T step into the elevator with me, the other guys staying down to secure the area.

"So now what?" I ask, flicking my gaze from Trey's reflection to T's.

T drapes a heavy arm across my shoulders. "Now we wait."

CHAPTER TWENTY-TWO

TREY

NOVEMBER 8TH

She paces from one side of the condo to the other, rich brownie colored hair floating in her wake. Fingers steepled beneath my chin, I track each of her movements while monitoring the TV plus the two computer screens set up along the coffee table.

Election Day.

"I'm going to puke," Randi says for the tenth time in the last hour. "Can someone ask that doctor lady to prescribe me some Xanax?"

Tank chuckles from the nest he set up hours ago. Candy wrappers litter the floor around the chair. He's a nervous eater, what can I say? "Come on now, Randi. We have hours left of this. Sit down, relax."

"Relax?" she screeches. I cringe at the sharp sound cutting into my eardrums. "I think I'm having a heart attack. What are the signs again?"

"Do not WebMD it," I say over the TV. "You're fine, Mess. I agree with Tank, sit your ass down."

"You two are the worst friends ever. I'll go die alone in my bedroom so I don't interrupt whatever you're doing which makes you too busy to be concerned about my failing health."

Wow. I roll my eyes to the ceiling. Sure as hell hope Randi's daughter didn't get her dramatics.

The bedroom door slams shut. Tank looks to the closed door, then back at me.

"Give her some time. She's fine," I mutter. "When do we need to leave for that watch party she has to attend?"

"Few hours from now. It'd be nice if we knew before we left. Not sure the partygoers are ready for that." He jerks a thumb over his shoulder toward the bedroom. "She's living up to the name you gave her."

I smirk and turn back to the screens. As the California numbers scroll across the bottom, the hairs on the back of my neck stand, a tingling feeling of being watched itching up my spine. Peeling my gaze from the screen, I meet Tank's dark eyes.

"Creeper. What?"

"How's that going?" He tilts his head back. "Ending it with her."

"Motherfucking terrible," I grit out. "I don't blame you though, if that's what you're worried about."

"I'm not. I'm worried about my friend, actually." *Aw, big guy has a big heart.* "I know how hard the shit with Rachel affected you. That's why I didn't stop you two, the flirting. For the first time in a year, you were acting normal. Don't let this drag you back down."

I sigh, lean back against the couch, and scrub a hand over my face. He's right about the gloom cloud that hung over my head after Rachel left me for Shawn. Even more right about Randi being the one to snap me out of it.

"I won't," I say after a beat.

"Don't let it distract you either."

"I know."

"Do not give me a reason to fire your ass, Trey." I whip my head to the right. "You know I'd have to if you break the rules, even if you are my best friend. Don't put me in that situation, got it?"

My chin dips in a minuscule nod.

I have to be strong and keep my hands off her if she wins. No, *when* she wins. I can't risk the entire team's job, her safety, and my relationship with my best friend. Even if staying away from her hurts like a motherfucking kick to the balls with a steel toe.

Part of me hopes they don't win; that way, I won't have to be around the one woman I want but can't have day after day. I'm already dreading the torture those four years will turn into.

But the other part wants her to win. To smear her success in the faces of all those fuckers who doubted her, who made fun of her as a kid. Hearing the long, detailed version of her childhood that day ripped my heart out of my chest, her tears shattering my one resolve to never kill for pleasure.

"I'll be fine."

No more untrue words were ever spoken.

BOISTEROUS CHEERS POUR out of the ballroom into the hallway where Tank and I stand stationed at the door. I catch his eye and smile.

"That's a good sign," I mutter, going back to scanning the long, empty halls for perceived threats.

"I've never wanted to know the outcome of an election more," he says with an annoyed huff. "Fucking killing me."

"Easy, big guy. We'll know soon enough."

Almost on cue, the doors fling open, a teary Randi marching through.

"We did it," she breathes, clapping her hands in front of her chest with a hop of pure joy. "We won." Midhop, she turns to Tank. "We won!"

"Congratulations, ma'am." True happiness warms his tone, tugging his lips in an almost smile. "Looking forward to the next four years."

"Me too, T. Me too." She turns back to face me, and her smile falters. My brows rise up my forehead. "Can I talk to you, in private?" She shoots a worried glance over her shoulder to the now-frowning Tank.

"Fine," he says like a parent would to a needy child. "Make it quick; I can't make excuses for too long. The bathrooms are down that way.

At least make it look like he's escorting you somewhere other than a dark corner."

Red flush spreads across her freckled cheeks. Ever since the press conference, she's dialed it back on the makeup and big hair, showing off more of her natural beauty.

I swing a hand out and bend at the waist in an exaggerated bow.

"Madam Vice President," I say with a smile.

Her lips spread wide. We walk side by side down the silent hall. "Wow, this is really happening," she says halfway to the bathroom sign. "Can you believe it?" Her shining eyes meet mine.

"I can. You deserve it, Mess. You and the people in this country deserve it. Someone like you has been a long time coming." I give my head a quick shake. "I can't wait to see what you do to this town. It might never be the same."

She snorts. "I sure the hell hope not. Now the real work starts, I guess." We pause outside the women's restroom. Her gaze flicks one way down the hall and then the other. "We haven't gotten a chance to talk... you know, about us and what's next."

The vulnerability in her voice shakes my soul, rattling the promise I made to Tank about staying away.

"That was then. You're the vice president elect of the United States of America. Things are different now. *You're* different."

Tears well in the corners of her eyes. Glancing up and down the hall, I grip her hand and tug her into a side door that leads to a large empty ballroom.

"Don't do that," I beg, my lips brushing against hers. "You're ripping me in two."

"I don't want it to end." Her voice catches. "Why can't we just keep sneaking around?"

"You deserve better than that, Mess. You know you do. And I need this solid line between us, both of us knowing that piece of us is tabled. Not over, just on hold." I tug her close, sealing her chest against my own. Lips in her hair, I kiss the top of her head. "Don't ask me to choose between you and this job, between you and Tank."

"I'm not. I swear I'm not. I'm just not ready for it to end. It's just started."

"I know, but it's not really over. I don't know if we ever could be."

Her shoulder shake, and I hold her tighter.

"Now what?" Lip trembling, eyes wet, she tilts her face up, eyes meeting mine.

The wet skin of her cheeks slides beneath my thumbs as I swipe away her tears. "Now... now we wait."

Trey and Randi's story continues in Power Twist– *Book 2 in the Power Play series.*
Swipe to read a sneak peek!

POWER TWIST SNEAK PEEK

RANDI

For a few seconds, neither of us says a word, building taut tension with each passing second. Like a magnet drawn to metal, an unseen force urges me closer to Trey until I'm almost toppling out of the chair right into him.

The past few months of staying apart, fighting this natural draw, have been hell. All I want is his calloused hands cupping my face and pulling me close. His lips sliding against my own while his fingers twist and pinch, creating the delicious torture I miss.

"Randi," Trey says reluctantly. His hot breath warms my cheek. I blink, pulling back an inch, surprised I'd gotten so close. "Please stop."

"Sorry," I mutter, righting myself back into the chair. I tuck my chin in the hope that Trey doesn't catch my embarrassed blush.

What the hell was I thinking? Burying my face deeper into the blanket, I shake my head. He said stop. My heart clenches as the word repeats in my mind. Maybe it isn't driving him crazy like it is me that we can't be together.

Per T, the lead of my Alpha secret service team, an agent 'mingling' with the VP is a big no-no. Though, I haven't found that particular rule documented in my research—yes, I've researched. Anyone would when it comes to the sexy-as-hell agent. Since T found us in bed together that morning, he's been adamant that the relationship Trey and I had started to form through the course of the campaign is over.

And it has been ever since that day.

Ugh, wallowing in this pitiful state does me no good. I need a distraction, to change topics, to choke on my own spit—anything to break the awkwardness surrounding us.

"Did you hear Kyle wants me at the White House tomorrow morning at eight?" I ask, my words muffled by the blanket. "He mentioned he has some topics I'll be interested in. Sounded fishy. When has Kyle ever helped me when he didn't have something to gain too?"

The chair tilts to the side and a groan of pain pierces the quiet as Trey shoves off the wicker to stand. Nose still tucked into the plaid blanket, I peer up to where Trey now leans with his back against a white decorative pole of the railing.

"What's he playing at?" he muses, his eyes fixed above my head, completely avoiding mine. "At least you don't have to wait long to know. Best to figure out his game plan and tackle it from there." He glances down at his watch. Lips pursed, he resituates his coat sleeve over his wrist. "I'm out of here in a few, and tomorrow's my day off. I won't be there—"

"It's okay," I say, attempting to put some strength into my voice. "I'll be fine. I can fill you and T in the next time I see you." I give him a dismissive wave beneath the thick blanket. "Go, have a good night." The tight, fake smile hurts my cheeks, my eyes burning with unshed tears.

Fuck, why does this hurt so much? Acting like his indifference, his rejection doesn't fucking slice me to the core. Because it does. Every step he moves away, the distance, every impersonal conversation wound my still-tender heart. The heart he softened with his sweet words and gentle touch all those scarce moments alone during the campaign.

"Randi—," he starts, empathy dripping in his soft tone, but cuts himself off with a muttered curse.

"Forget it," I bite out. Palms digging into the thin wooden rods, I shove out of the chair, the blanket pooling around my light gray Uggs. "See you when I see you," I toss over my shoulder as I hurry inside the house before the pooling tears can spill over.

You'd think after two months of this cold side of Trey, I'd be immune to it by now. But nope, it still hurts.

T shoots me a confused glance as I rush past him toward the stairs. His mouth opens, readying to say something, but I stop him with a hard look. I shouldn't be annoyed at him, but he's the cause of my current pain. He's the one who halted the one relationship I can't get enough of, keeping me away from the one man I crave.

I make it halfway up the stairs when a lone tear escapes to drip down my cheek. I hastily wipe it away with the back of my hand before it's visible on the security cameras for all the agents to see. The bedroom door bangs shut behind me as I storm toward the bathroom.

Hands gripping the marble vanity top, I hang my head. Every night, every day has been the same heartrending agony. Seeing him, wanting him, and not having him. Of his casual smiles, easy laughs, and cold touches. At least I only have to endure this cruel form of soul-crushing torture for 1,460 more days.

Fuck. Me.

Download Power Twist to find out what happens next!
Power Twist

ALSO BY KENNEDY L. MITCHELL

Standalone:

Falling for the Chance

A Covert Affair

Finding Fate

Memories of Us

Protection Series: Interconnected Standalone

Mine to Protect

Mine to Save

Mine to Guard (Coming April 2021)

More Than a Threat Series: A Bodyguard Romantic Suspense

More Than a Threat

More Than a Risk

More Than a Hope (Coming June 2021)

Power Play Series: A Protector Romantic Suspense

Power Games

Power Twist

Power Switch

Power Surge

Power Term

ACKNOWLEDGMENTS

There are so many people who made this series possible. First and foremost my two best friends, my tribe, my cheerleaders and alpha readers - Em and Chris, Thank you. You two are, AGH, there are no words for to thank you both enough for all that you do. From the encouraging texts to the slight realignment of the story to keeping my crass ass from being, well, too crass. I wouldn't be doing this without you. You two are the reason I write and still continue loving this crazy adventure.

Thank you to Hot Tree Editing - especially Kristin my amazing editor. Working with you is a DREAM. Thank you for all that you do to make my manuscripts shine.

Of course the bloggers who read the super duper advanced copies of PP and all those who read it now. This book would be no where without you. What you bring to the indie publishing community is priceless. Thank you for everything you do from reading, writing detailed reviews, and posting the billion teasers. So much of my success is directly linked to you.

Emilie at InkSlinger, thank you for helping me plan out the release schedule! It was so daunting until I worked side by side with you to plan out these five books. Thank you.

And of course Book Nerd Services, who hands down have helped change the course of my career. Thank you for all your hard work and countless PM's. You two are rockstars in my book.

And last but not least, to you the reader. Thank you for taking a chance on a no name author. Every time I see a page read or a book sale my heart thumps with happiness. I love sharing my stories with you and hope you love my crazy friends too.

Printed in Great Britain
by Amazon

40095924R00126